2

LOVING A COWBOY

GLORIA DOTY

Love can find you at any age.

Gloria Doty

Cover Design by Gwen Gades
Edited by Nina Newton

ISBN 978-1533326058

Acknowledgments

As with the first book, *Bring a Cowboy Home,* I consulted friends and acquaintances who had expertise in fields where my own knowledge was not sufficient or was seriously lacking.

They graciously and generously shared their knowledge and therefore made it much easier to write this book.

Medical: Kathy Sias-Head
Adoption Regulations: Andrea Pellerin Requenes
Rehab House: Kendra Wheeler
Chicago: Nancy Humphrey Haskins
Firearms: Todd Radke
Horses: Diane Butler Radke
Investments: Melinda Woll
Home Births: Melanie Hull
I also want to thank my amazing TEAM:
Nina Newton, Editor
Gwen Gades, Cover Designer
Pat Spence, Proofreader
Heather Huffman: Marketing Manager
Becki Brannen: Project Manager

I dedicate all my writing to my Lord and Savior, Jesus Christ, who grants me courage and blesses my efforts.

This book is also dedicated to my friends and relatives who have supported me in my writing endeavors. They have been encouraging and truthful. They gave of their time and energy and always provided feedback.

I especially want to thank Patti and Barbara and Shirley. These three friends read every chapter as soon as it was written. They would encourage me to keep writing as they wanted to read the "next" chapter. Their comments always made me smile and forced me to keep writing.

Chapter 1

"GRAMMA LUCY, GRAMMA LUCY. Wake up. Grandpa says you are a sleepyhead. Come on."

Lucy opened one eye; Cal's 5-year-old granddaughter, Amy, had her face so close it was nearly touching her nose.

"Amy, why are you up so early? Let Gramma sleep a little longer."

"No-o-o, Gramma. Come on. Grandpa's making monkey pancakes."

Lucy opened both eyes and looked over her shoulder where her husband of two months was supposed to be. No Cal. She sighed, swung her legs over the side of the bed and grabbed her summer robe.

Amy took her hand and pulled her to the kitchen.

"See, Gramma? I told you Grandpa was making monkey pancakes."

Lucy moved closer to the stove where Cal was standing at the griddle with a spatula in his hand and grinning at her.

"Monkey pancakes…really? Are you showing off since we both know I can't make regular pancakes without setting off the smoke alarm?" she asked him.

Cal smiled and continued to use a squeeze bottle to put batter on the griddle in the shape of a monkey's face.

"I'm impressed, Love. Where did you learn to do that?" Lucy asked.

"Pinterest."

Lucy's eyes grew wide, and she started laughing. Somehow her 6'4" rugged rancher husband didn't fit her idea of the typical Pinterest person.

Intrigued, she asked, "Where did you hear about Pinterest?"

"I heard Samantha talking about it, so I thought I'd check it out. That's when I saw these monkey pancakes. I knew the kids would like 'em. Besides, a guy has to stay on top of things, y'know."

Lucy moved closer to him and rubbed her body lightly against his arm. "You do a good job of that, Cowboy."

Cal winked at her and put another pancake on Amy's plate. Looking at Lucy, he asked, "Why don't you put butter and syrup on that for Amy before you get us both in trouble?"

While she helped Amy, Lucy thought making pancakes was one more thing she would add to the list of information she was learning about this man she loved so much. They had only known each other six months before they were married. There were new things she learned every day, and so far, they were all positive.

There was a knock on the door that led to the great room which was situated between their house and the living quarters on the opposite end of the ranch house. Amy ran to open the door.

"Uncle Ben!" she yelled as she jumped up to wrap her arms around his neck. "Come in and have monkey pancakes with me," she begged as she pulled him to the table.

Ben gave Lucy a questioning look.

She shrugged her shoulders. "Just one more of your father's many talents he didn't tell me about before I married him." In a more serious voice, she asked, "How's Candy feeling this morning?"

Ben shook his head. "Not good. She wouldn't even let me make coffee. She said the smell was going to send her back to the bathroom. I tucked her in on the couch, left some crackers and water on the end table, and thought I'd come over here and beg a cup of coffee."

Amy, who listened much too intently to conversations between her mother, Cal's daughter Samantha, and her Aunt Jackie, piped up. "Is Aunt Candy going to have a baby today, Uncle Ben?"

"No, Sweetie. Not for a long time yet, but she doesn't feel very good this morning."

Satisfied with that answer, she asked, "Do you want some pancakes? Grandpa will make some for you. Won't you, Grandpa?"

Cal put a stack of pancakes in front of Ben, while Lucy poured a cup of coffee for him.

"Thanks, Dad. I have to say I'm impressed with the monkey faces." Ben laughed and continued, "I also came to ask what time you were planning on leaving this morning."

Cal glanced at the mess he had made in the kitchen and told Ben, "Give me an hour, okay?"

Ben, with his mouth full, nodded. "That's good. I'll take Amy to the barn with me to feed the horses, and then we'll stop at our house so she can say hello to Candy. Why don't you come get me when you're ready to go?"

Lucy told Cal, "I'll clean up the dishes. My talent in the kitchen lies in the clean-up part of cooking. But I'm going to take a shower and get dressed first." She kissed him lightly on the cheek and left.

Cal watched her go, her lightweight robe not doing a very good job of hiding the strong, supple body under it.

God, I don't know why you blessed me with that woman, but I will thank you every day for the rest of my life, he thought.

* * *

Lucy stepped out of the shower, wrapped an over-sized towel around herself, and used a smaller one to dry her hair. As she scrutinized her reflection in the mirror, she touched the few streaks of gray that were mixed in with her dark hair. *Was it time to color it? Would Cal like it better if it were all dark?* Her hand touched the scar on her cheek, an ever-present reminder of a dangerous night when she still lived and worked in Chicago, before she moved back to Texas and married Cal.

In the mirror, she saw Cal come into the bathroom and stand behind her. She turned to him, putting her hands on his chest. "Cal, will you love me when my hair is completely gray and my skin is nothing but wrinkles?"

"Lucy, I will love you no matter what color your hair is, and I don't see any wrinkles and I never will."

She reveled in his answer, then asked, "Where's Amy?"

"Ben took her with him. I'm supposed to find him when I'm ready to leave."

"How soon are you leaving?"

He gently tugged on her towel and let it drop to the floor.

"Not for a little while."

* * *

After Cal and Ben left for Houston, Lucy went to find Amy. She knocked softly on Candy's door before opening it a crack to peek inside. Candy smiled and motioned for her to come in. Amy was stretched out on the couch, napping, with her head on Candy's lap.

Lucy laughed. "That's what happens when you get up at the crack of dawn and eat a whole stack of pancakes with syrup. That sugar high bottoms out pretty fast."

"Is that what happened?" Candy said, nodding her head. "I wondered why she was so tired this early in the morning."

"I hope Ben isn't napping on the way to town. He ate a stack of them, too."

Candy smiled and told Lucy, "I feel so bad for Ben. This morning sickness is killing me and making his life miserable, too. This morning I wouldn't even let him make coffee. It should have been over a few months ago. I don't know why it still hits me sometimes."

Lucy looked at her daughter-in-law and remembered feeling like that before she had her daughter, Victoria. Thinking about Vicki, she remembered she needed to call her as soon as she went back to her end of the house.

"I know I'm miserable at this stage of pregnancy, but how is Vicki doing?" Candy asked.

"Truthfully, she's pretty miserable too, but part of that is due to her impatience. She has several weeks before her due date, but you'd think she was a month *overdue*. I'm going to stay at their house with Bethany and Devon when she goes to the hospital and possibly for a few days after she gets home. Having three children under the age of 4 is a bit more than they anticipated when she and David made the decision to adopt. They were thrilled to be able to have two children immediately but never dreamed they would have a baby so soon, too."

"Ben and I wanted to wait a little longer before we started a family, but I guess the Lord had other plans," Candy said as she lovingly ran her hand over her belly.

"I hope you and Ben have a dozen, Candy. This ranch house needs all the bedrooms filled with sweet, noisy munchkins."

Candy looked at her dubiously. "I'm thinking maybe two, Lucy. That's a long way from a dozen, but it might be enough."

Candy stroked Amy's forehead, softly brushing the hair out of her eyes. "Why don't we let Amy sleep, and I'll send her over when she wakes up."

Lucy nodded. "If you feel like any food by lunchtime, I'll bring something over. It won't be nearly as exciting as monkey pancakes, but it will taste good. I promise."

* * *

Lucy walked through the great room, thinking, *Maybe I should check Pinterest for a recipe.* Then she laughed out loud. *Calvin Frasier, I love you so much. You never fail to amaze me.*

She found the two plastic tubs she had asked Cal to bring down from an upstairs bedroom. Unless visitors needed a place to spend the night, one of the rooms above the great room was used more for storage than as a bedroom. The containers were filled with photographs.

She sat on the floor to look at the photos in the first tub. These were her family albums. She spread them out in front of her. Her great-grandparents looked back at her from a posed sepia-colored print. The subjects in that generation's photos always looked so grim. There was never a glimmer of a smile. The next one was a picture of her beloved grandparents, Ivy and Herman Henderson, who raised her and her brother. They were standing in front of the ranch house. It was the Yellow Rose Ranch at that time. The next photo was of her parents, Albert and Selma. They were smiling. Her mother held her baby brother, Leon, while Lucy was sitting on her father's lap. She looked like she was about 3 years old so Leon would have been 1. That must have been taken a year before her parents were both killed when the small plane her father was piloting exploded in mid-air.

Lucy scrutinized the photo. Did she resemble her mother? No, she didn't think so. She did, however, look like a mirror image of her father. Perhaps that was the reason Grandpa spent so much time teaching her "boy" things like riding, roping calves, shooting a revolver, and playing poker. She reminded him of the son he lost way too soon, and she obviously became a replacement for her father in Grandpa's life.

Well, Grandpa, those skills have stood me in good stead over the years. I'm forever grateful for the things you taught me. Her fingers unconsciously felt for the scar on her cheek.

CHAPTER 2

LUCY WAS STILL SORTING THROUGH THE PICTURES when Amy came into the room and joined her, plopping down on the floor beside her.

"Who are all the people in these pictures, Gramma?"

Lucy picked up one from the second tub. It was a photo of Cal's mother and father. His sister was a baby, and he was standing by his father, trying to look grown up. "This little boy is your Grandpa Cal, Amy."

Amy laughed at the thought of her grandpa being a child. Lucy sifted through the pile until she found a family picture of Cal and his first wife, Kathy. Their three children were placed strategically around them. Pointing to Samantha, Lucy told her, "Amy, this little girl is your mom, that's your Aunt Jackie, and this baby is your Uncle Ben."

Amy held it and looked at it for a long time. "Who is that with Grandpa?"

"That is your mommy's mom. She got sick and is in heaven with Jesus now. That was before you were born, Sweetheart. Look, Amy. Here's another picture of your mommy when she was about your age."

They looked through a few more piles of pictures. "This is a picture of me and my brother and our parents," Lucy told her.

Amy suddenly remembered something. "Mommy said you lived here when you were a little girl. Is that true?"

"Yes, I did. My mom and dad and my baby brother and I lived in the part of the ranch house where Uncle Ben and Aunt Candy live now. My grandparents lived in the part where Grandpa Cal and I live now."

Lucy could still remember the day her parents were killed. She and Leon had stayed with Grandma and Grandpa while their parents went to Dallas to pick up the repaired plane. Only they never came home. Days later, without much explanation, Grandpa moved all of her and Leon's clothes and toys out of their house and into the house on the other end. If she closed her eyes, she could see herself dragging her stuffed rabbit across the great room to her new home. She was only 4 years old and didn't understand why her mommy and daddy didn't come back.

"Gramma Lucy, are you sad?" Amy asked.

"Maybe a little, Amy. Looking at pictures makes us remember things, and sometimes that can make us sad. Let's get these pictures cleaned up. I will find frames for some of them, and perhaps the next time you visit you can help me hang them on that big empty wall over there, okay? Then you can look at the pictures any time you're here."

* * *

When Cal and Ben returned much later in the day, Lucy had dinner ready for them. She sent Amy to get Candy so they could all eat together.

"I saw a picture of you when you were a baby, Uncle Ben, and one of you, too, Grandpa. Gramma says I can help her hang them all on the wall."

Ben laughed and said, "I've seen my baby pictures, and I certainly hope our baby looks like you, Candy."

Cal smiled and shook his head. "Ben, as I recall, you were a very cute baby. I hope your baby looks just like you…if it's a boy, of course."

After Cal tucked Amy into bed and said prayers with her, he joined Lucy who was already in bed. She snuggled up against him and voiced something that had been going around in her head since the afternoon.

"Cal, what do you think about having a headstone made with my parents' names on it? Nothing big or fancy; in fact, both their names could be on one headstone. We could put it by Grandma and Grandpa's stones in the little plot by the cabin."

"That's fine with me, Honey. What made you think of that? The pictures?"

"Yes, I suppose so. I think I never had closure after they died. It was such a violent explosion, there was nothing to bury, so I guess Grandma and Grandpa didn't purchase a marker. I know that sounds strange now, but I believe they were in shock and utter disbelief and suddenly, at 61 years old, they had two babies to raise. It probably wasn't something that mattered then. Grandma always said she had my parents in her heart, but I think I need it…for me. You know, some tangible evidence they lived…and died."

Cal kissed the top of her head. "When you have time, draw a sketch of what you would like to have written. You might want to ask Leon's opinion. We'll check on it the next time we're in Tomball, okay?"

Suddenly Lucy remembered the reason Cal and Ben went to Houston. "I forgot to ask. What information did you get at the meeting?"

"I'll tell you about our day in the morning, at breakfast."

Cal had his arm around Lucy's shoulders. She placed her head on his chest and listened to the rhythm of his heartbeat and his slow, steady breathing long after he fell asleep.

Please protect this man you brought into my life, Lord. He is everything to me, and I can't imagine life without him.

* * *

When Cal came to breakfast the next morning, Amy was already eating a bowl of cold cereal. There was a plate of bagels and a bowl of fruit on the table.Lucy looked at Cal. Without blinking, she said, "What? You expected bacon and eggs? I found this recipe on Pinterest. It was on a board titled, 'Easy Breakfasts for Busy Grandmothers.'" She started laughing and couldn't stop.

Cal poured cereal into his bowl, added milk, and shook his head. "You are so bad, Lucy."

"I know it, and you love me that way, don't you, Cowboy?" She moved around behind him, put her arms around his neck and nibbled on his earlobe. "I'm sorry. I couldn't resist after your monkey pancakes yesterday. I promise I will make something spectacular for dinner tonight. At least, as spectacular as it gets when it's my cooking."

She moved to the counter and poured a cup of coffee for each of them. As she sat back down, she asked, "What did you find out yesterday? Did you meet the ranger in charge of this county?"

"No. It seems he was transferred to another location, and there isn't a replacement yet. They're hoping there will be soon. Since we already made the trip, we didn't want the day to be a total loss, so we looked at ATVs. Ben is certain they would be more efficient than horses alone when moving cattle."

"From the tone of your voice, I'm assuming you don't agree with him?"

"Lucy, I think perhaps I'm feeling my age. I like the traditional, you know that. In my head, cattle ought to be herded by men," he paused for a second, "or women, on horseback, not by someone on a glorified toy."

Lucy rubbed his shoulders. "I would never say you were getting old, Cal. Progress is always difficult to accept, no matter what age we are. Did you and Ben reach an agreement?"

Cal laughed. "I guess you could call it that. The dealership is delivering two ATVs next week."

"You are such a softie, Calvin Frasier. That's one of the many things I love about you."

Cal pulled her around in front of him and onto his lap. "Maybe when they're delivered, we can each get on one and take off for the far reaches of the ranch before anybody knows we're gone."

"Well, we wouldn't have to feed or water them or worry about them getting tired, but we might run out of gas."

"That sounds like a good idea, too," he chuckled as he pulled her to him and kissed her.

Lucy reluctantly stood up and told Amy. "Okay, Sweetie, if you're done with breakfast, let's get your things packed. You can say good-bye to Uncle Ben and Aunt Candy, and then we're meeting your mom so you can go home."

"No-o-o-o. Don't make me go home. I want to stay here. Please, Grandpa. Please, Gramma Lucy."

"Amy, why don't you want to go home? Your parents and brother are missing you."

"No, they're not. I want to stay because you and Grandpa kiss each other, and all Mommy and Daddy do is yell at each other. All the time. Then Daddy leaves and slams the door, and Mommy cries. Don't make me go back, please."

Lucy looked at Cal and frowned. He shrugged his shoulders, indicating he had no idea what was going on.

"Do you have plans for lunch today, Cal?" Lucy asked.

He shook his head, understanding Lucy wanted him to take Amy back so he could possibly speak to his daughter and find out what was happening. He asked Amy, "How about this? Grandpa will take you to meet your mom, and we'll have lunch at the restaurant where you like the slides and tunnels, okay?"

Amy reluctantly nodded her head. "Okay, I guess."

Cal and Lucy knew Samantha, Cal's daughter, would be much more likely to confide in her father rather than Lucy, since she was the most vocal about her opposition to their marriage in the beginning. Although she accepted Lucy in Cal's life now and was always friendly, this might be a subject she would be more comfortable discussing with her father.

* * *

While Cal was gone, Lucy called her best friend, Phoebe. They hadn't spoken for over a week, which was unusual.

"Hi Phoebe. It's good to hear your voice. We haven't talked for a while."

"Lucy, I'm sorry I haven't called. I've been pretty busy."

"It's okay. There seems to have been a grandchild or two here every day anyway. Is the printing business keeping you busy?"

"Yes, among other things," Phoebe said, laughing.

"Phoebe Reynolds, what are you not telling me? I know that tone in your voice. What are you up to?"

Phoebe laughed as only she could. "I knew you would know, Lucy. The truth is I've been seeing a lot of Jerry."

"Jerry? As in Jerry the attorney? As in Jerry from Texas? As in our friend Jerry?" Lucy's voice rose an octave with each question.

Phoebe continued to chuckle. "Yep. That's the one. We've been seeing quite a bit of each other ever since you introduced us at the 'painting party' at Vicki's house last fall. He has meetings in Chicago occasionally, and when he does, he calls me and we meet somewhere for dinner or the evening."

Lucy's thoughts got stuck on "the evening" but she didn't want to sound like Cal's daughters had, so she didn't pursue that train of thought. Besides, she knew Phoebe would never consider spending the night with any man for fear of revealing her past physical and emotional scars. And, she was definitely old enough to make her own choices without any advice from Lucy.

"Wow. That's over six months ago. Why haven't you told me? Now my feelings are hurt," Lucy pouted. "I didn't realize Jerry had that much business in Illinois."

Phoebe giggled when she answered. "Truthfully, I think sometimes he wouldn't have to fly here, but he does anyway, and I'm sorry I didn't tell you, Lucy. It started out as just friends meeting for lunch or dinner and interesting conversation, but lately it has taken a turn to the serious side, and I'm scared to death."

"Oh Phoebe, I am so happy for you! Isn't it great to feel wanted and alive and loved?"

"Whoa, Sister. You know me better than anyone on earth does. I didn't say anything about love. I'm just enjoying the attention and friendship. I'm not looking for my cowboy like you were. I don't want to live in Texas, and I'm pretty sure Jerry isn't going to move his practice to Chicago. Besides, there are lots of things about me he doesn't know, and unlike you, I intend to keep it that way."

They talked for a while longer, catching up on family news. Lucy told her about Cal's idea to ride the ATVs when they arrived and about Vicki being ready to have the baby, the sooner, the better.

Lucy did know her friend better than anyone. She knew Phoebe was lonesome and even more so since Lucy moved away. While she was thrilled about the relationship with Jerry, she also knew when Phoebe found the right man, she might fall hard for him, but she would never allow herself to be *with* him. That thought made Lucy sad for Phoebe and maybe for Jerry, too.

* * *

When Cal returned, Lucy asked, "What did Samantha have to say when you met her?"

"At first, she denied anything was wrong, but when I told her what Amy said, she cried and said Sean had moved out and was going to file for a separation. I asked if she could tell me what caused it, but she said she didn't know for sure. She thinks he's having an affair with some woman at work. I felt so bad for her. I did ask her to come to church with us on Sunday and then stay for dinner. I'm sorry I didn't check with you first."

"That's no problem. We'll rustle up some grub." She laughed the throaty laugh Cal loved to hear. "See? I can talk like one of them thar ranch hands."

Chapter 3

"CAL, HOW DO YOU FEEL about me making a short trip to Denver to talk to Leon about the headstone? I checked for flights. I could leave tomorrow and return on Thursday. I know it would be a short visit, but I'm really going just to ask him about the tombstone. I would love for you to go with me, depending on how busy you are. Vicki's doctor said it would be at least a week or two before the baby comes. I know babies make their own plans, but if she has it early, Ben and Candy could help you watch Devon and Bethany until I could make arrangements to get back. If you have to, send Simon and his plane to get me."

Cal listened to this barrage of information and laughed at his wife. "How long have you had this idea in your head, Lucy?"

"Not long…since you left with Amy this morning, actually. I spoke to Phoebe for a bit and then checked for flights. Why?"

"Because you seem to have every detail worked out. You are the efficient one, aren't you?"

"Is that a compliment or a complaint? If you would rather I didn't go, I'll be fine with that. I can go after the baby is here. You know me; when I have an idea, I think I need to act on it immediately."

He reached for her and kissed her first, then said, "I never have a complaint about you, Lucy, but I don't think I can leave right now. Please tell Leon I said hello, okay? What time do I need to have you at the airport in the morning?"

* * *

Leon's wife, Ginny, was waiting for Lucy when she arrived at the airport in Loveland, Colorado. Leon worked at a rehab center in Loveland, and they had purchased a home there, too.

"Are you tired, Lucy? If not, we can stop by the center where Leon works. He would love to introduce you to his co-workers. I believe he has a surprise for you, too," she added quietly.

"That would be great, Ginny. It was a pleasant flight, and I definitely am not tired."

Surprises have never been high on my hit parade. They usually are not good in my experience, Lucy thought.

Ginny parked in the drive of a lovely older home in a residential neighborhood. There were shade trees dotting the lawn and beautiful flowers blooming along the walk. The only indication it was anything other than a family home was the small wooden sign in the front yard with the words, *The Mountain House* carved into it.

A young man answered the door. "Hello. I'm Troy. You must be Leon's sister. I can see the resemblance. He's in here."

He led them down a hallway with offices on either side. Ginny said she would wait in the living room. Troy knocked, and Leon opened the door.

"Hello Lucy," he said as he engulfed her in a hug. "I can't tell you how happy I am to see you. Ginny says I haven't stopped smiling since you called to ask if you could visit for a few days." He looked over her shoulder. "Is Cal with you?"

"No, not this time. He had a lot of things to do at the ranch, but he did tell me to tell you hello."

Leon nodded in understanding. "Let me show you around my little work world."

He led the way around the house-turned-rehab-center. Some of the bedrooms had been turned into offices, but the majority of the house looked exactly as it had when it was someone's home. A large kitchen and living room plus two baths were on the first floor with bedrooms and baths upstairs. There was an activities room in the finished basement where the residents could watch television, play pool, or exercise.

"So, how do the men find this place, Leon?" Lucy asked.

"They have to be referred by a doctor, hospital, or the court system. If someone would wander in off the street, we'd find another facility for them. A hospital in downtown Denver sent me here when I was found on the street, nearly dead. It didn't seem like it at the time, but that was quite possibly the luckiest day of my life. Until I met Ginny, of course," he added.

The tour had come full circle, and they were back in the living room with Ginny. Leon glanced at her, and when she smiled and nodded at him, he continued. "I have another person I would like you to meet, Lucy."

He led the way to a spacious office. The placard on the door had the words, Pastor Clint Henderson, engraved on it.

"Lucy, I'd like you to meet Clint, my son and your nephew. Clint, this is my sister, Lucy Frasier."

Lucy knew her eyebrows must have shot up about 2 inches. She shook hands with the man in front of her. "Forgive me if I look surprised, Clint. I'm sure you know this is quite a shock…not an unpleasant one…but a shock, nonetheless."

When he smiled, he did indeed look like Leon. "I'm sure it is. I asked my father if you had a strong heart, since he insisted on surprising you with my existence."

"I'm glad I passed that test, but I know y'all aren't going to leave me hanging now. I want to hear the rest of the story."

Oh my goodness, Lucy, did you just say y'all? Nothing like acting like the stereotypical Texan, she told herself.

"Yes, you will hear the rest of the story tonight at dinner. Clint and his wife are going to join us. Be prepared for a scrumptious meal. I married an excellent cook," Leon told her.

They said their goodbyes, and Ginny drove the few miles through town to her and Leon's house. It was a small home in a quiet neighborhood. Lucy felt at home the minute she stepped in the door. It was light and breezy with pastel walls and white furniture. Ginny showed her to the spare bedroom and told her to make herself at home.

"I think I will talk to you while you prepare dinner, if that's okay."

"Sure," Ginny said, "as long as you don't critique my skills. Leon exaggerates my cooking abilities sometimes."

Lucy laughed out loud. "Oh Ginny, you have no idea how funny that is. I have a very limited number of cooking skills, so you will get no advice from me. Although I can peel vegetables or something simple like that if you need me to."

Ginny seemed surprised. "Really? I thought you probably learned all those things from your grandmother. Leon says she was a great cook."

"He's right, she was an outstanding cook. I learned to make delicious, flaky biscuits and Texas chili that will knock your socks off, but that's about the extent of any culinary masterpieces. I never wanted to sit still long enough to learn. I was too busy learning things from Grandpa."

Ginny asked Lucy what she would prefer to be called, Lucy or Louisa. "You can call me either one, Ginny. Believe it or not, when Leon was a toddler, he called me Luli. Fortunately, when he could talk a little better, he changed it to

Lucy. Business associates knew me as Louisa, friends and family usually call me Lucy, and I allow Cal to call me Lucy Mae, but no one else."

They visited while Ginny worked her magic in the kitchen. She told Lucy she had never had any children. She hadn't even considered marrying until she met Leon and fell head over heels in love with him.

Lucy asked, "Did you know about his past and addictions when you met him?"

"Not immediately, but he told me on our second date. He said he had enough secrets in his life; he wasn't going to keep anything from me." She continued, "The one thing I didn't know, and he didn't either, was that he had fathered a son. But I'll let him tell you about that."

They spent the rest of the day talking about the benefits of living in Colorado and about Ginny's family. Even though Ginny had attended their wedding, Lucy re-introduced her to her and Cal's families with some pictures she brought with her.

Leon left work early and walked in with a bouquet of flowers for Ginny. He kissed her and told her how much he loved her. While Ginny arranged the flowers in a vase for a centerpiece on the dinner table, Leon sat with Lucy.

"I would like to tell you about Clint before he gets here. Several years ago, a woman called and asked to come see me. She said it was important. I had no idea what she wanted or who she was, but I was intrigued so I agreed to meet her. When I opened the door, I immediately recognized a pretty woman from my drinking and gambling days. She was older, of course, as was I, but she looked the same. She told me I had a son, fathered on one of our drunken escapades. She had never looked for me and had raised him by herself, but now she had cancer and was only expected to live for possibly another six months. She wanted me to know about him and for him to know his father before she died. She had never had any other children or any other close relatives, and she didn't want to leave him with no family. He wasn't a child, obviously. He was a grown man, but she felt it was necessary for him to know he had some family in this world. I was going to ask to take a paternity test, but when I saw his picture, I couldn't deny he was my son. To say our first meeting was awkward is an understatement of great magnitude." Leon smiled remembering that momentous occasion.

He continued, "We had some long talks. It was, perhaps, a little easier because he was an adult. He could understand how things, like the night of his conception, can happen. I wish his mother had let me know him sooner. I missed so much of his life and perhaps I could have helped her financially, although not until I was in rehab and had a steady job." Leon paused for a minute, lost in thought. "It doesn't matter now. It is what it is. His mother did die, and I am thankful she contacted me before that happened. He was already a minister when we met. When there was a position open at the center, I asked if he would be interested. I thought he would be able to relate to men in situations similar to his own. He accepted, and here we are."

When Clint arrived, he introduced Lucy to his wife, Janet. They all gathered in the living room to visit before dinner. Lucy observed Clint and Leon's interactions. It made her happy to know her brother was happy.

True to Leon's predictions, dinner was delicious. "My compliments to the chef, Ginny. I wish I had paid attention to Grandma so I could create a meal like that. Now if you want to throw a deck of cards and some poker chips on the table, I'll show you what I learned instead."

The second the words were out of her mouth, Lucy was apologizing. "I am so sorry, Leon. That was a terribly insensitive thing to say to a recovered gambling addict. Obviously, I haven't lost my ability to put my mouth in gear before my brain is engaged. Please forgive me."

Leon was shaking his head. "There's no need to apologize, Lucy. I have no problem with talking about my past because I don't live there any longer. There is not one thing from my past, with the exception of Clint, of course, that has any hold on me. God granted me a new life, a loving wife, a son, a fulfilling job, and there is nothing else I need. My life is here. I would not return to my former life, under any circumstances. All the mistakes I made and the problems I caused are gone from my mind, wiped clean by the blood of Jesus. That day in Illinois, when you said you forgave me for losing the Yellow Rose, was the last day I thought about my past. I am a forgiven sinner, and I try to live my life as one."

Lucy knew she wasn't to that point yet in her life. She did slip into the past occasionally, and she obviously still held the Yellow Rose very close to her heart.

The others moved outside to enjoy the beautiful evening.

It was as though Leon read her mind. He leaned forward and took her hands. "Luli, listen to me. You married a really good man. He has tried to give your childhood back to you the only way he knows how. He bought a horse like the one you had when you were a child, he named a small piece of land the Yellow Rose, and he even gave you a yellow diamond for an engagement ring. Nothing Cal can do will bring back our parents or our childhood or the Yellow Rose. We are both adults, and it is time to move on and enjoy our new lives. There's a difference between enjoying your memories and clinging fiercely to them. Do you believe that?"

Lucy had tears on her lashes, threatening to run down her cheeks. "I understand it in my head, Leon, but my heart just won't let go completely. I don't know what it will take for me to be completely free."

He handed her a tissue and gave her a hug. "Come on, that's enough serious talking for one night. Let's join the rest of the family on the patio. I've taken tomorrow off so Ginny and I can show you some of our beautiful scenery here in Colorado before your flight back to Texas." They moved outside, and Lucy became better acquainted with her nephew and his wife. After some reminiscing and telling stories about things that happened while they were kids, Ginny served dessert and coffee.

Shortly after, Clint and Janet left, and Lucy went to bed, still hearing Leon's words in her head.

* * *

They stopped at a small café for lunch the next day while on their sightseeing trip. Lucy had almost forgotten the reason she came to Colorado.

"I know we need to move on, Leon, and I agree with what you said; however, the reason I came for a one-day visit was to ask you about a marker for our parents. I would like to place a small stone with their names on it in the same place where Grandma and Grandpa are buried. I need to have something that says they lived and died. Right now, it seems as though they never existed. I thought a lot about what you said last night. Maybe I am still that 4-year-old girl waiting for her parents to come home. There was never any closure there. We just moved in with Grandma and Grandpa, and life went on as if nothing happened."

"I think you're probably right, Lucy. I was so young, I can barely remember it, so I don't think it affected me like it affected you. You certainly have my blessing to have a marker made. I would like to see pictures when it's set in the ground. You can design it any way you'd like, Lucy. I will pay for half, and one day Ginny and I will come to see it."

CHAPTER 4

WEEKS LATER, after her parents' headstone was ordered, Lucy told Cal she was going to the cabin to spend a few hours in peaceful reminiscing and meditation and deciding where she wanted it to be placed. He asked if she wanted Harmony saddled or if she was riding bareback today, although he already knew the answer.

"I don't need the saddle, Honey. I feel more peaceful with my memories when I ride bareback. I won't be gone too long. I'll be back before dinner."

"Do you have everything you need?"

Lucy smiled at him. "Phone, check. Grandma's Bible, check. Revolver, check. Yep. Everything but the love of my life, and I know where you are."

She rode slowly, enjoying the solitude and peacefulness. It was warm but not unbearably hot yet. When she arrived at the cabin, she took Harmony to the lean-to but stopped short when she saw the dirt floor was covered with evidence of other horses having been there…recently. She had her revolver in her hand and stayed as still as possible, listening for voices or the sound of horses moving. When she was certain there was no one in the vicinity, she knelt down to examine the tracks. It appeared to be three riders; the heaviest one was on a horse that was missing a shoe on the right hind hoof.

Lucy used her phone to take pictures of the place she thought would be best for placement of the headstone, all the while staying alert for any noises or movement. When she was finished, she cautiously opened the front door of the cabin. She almost cried when she saw the mess. Someone had been using the cabin Cal built as a gift to her, for a rendezvous point…but for what? She closed the door without touching anything, signaled for Harmony to come to her and then rode home.

Cal was surprised to see Lucy riding back so soon. He grabbed Harmony's bridle and let Lucy slip off.

"What's going on, Lucy? I thought you were going to stay for a while. What happened?"

Before she could answer, two men came riding up the long drive. Cal greeted the oldest one. "Hello, Sheriff. What are you doing way out here and on horseback, at that? I usually see you in your truck."

"Hi Cal. We're in the vicinity checking with ranchers to see if they've had any cattle go missing lately. By the way, this is Deputy Dawson. He's new in the county."

Cal reached up and shook the deputy's hand. "Deputy. Nice to meet you."

Cal introduced both men to Lucy, "This is my wife, Louisa."

Sheriff Ganger smiled and touched the brim of his hat. "Hello, ma'am." Turning to Cal, he said, "I heard you got yourself hitched, Cal. Congratulations."

Lucy never took her eyes off the deputy nor his horse. When he rode up, she noticed his horse was favoring the right hind leg. Deputy Dawson was looking at her, also, but not in a way she appreciated. He was in his late 30s, perhaps, and would have been a terribly handsome man if it weren't for the sneer that seemed permanently etched on his face.

"I'll ask Ben if he's seen any signs of rustling, but I'm certain he would've told me if he had. I'll make sure to tell my foreman to be on the lookout, okay? Lucy was on the east quarter fence line a bit ago. Did you notice anything strange, Honey?"

"Nope, not a thing," she lied. She would tell Cal about it later but not with Deputy *Dawg* here.

The two men turned and rode down the drive.

When they were out of earshot, Cal turned to her. "Do you want to tell me what's going on?"

"When I got to the cabin, someone had been there. Three riders from the looks of the tracks in the lean-to. The heaviest one is riding a horse that has thrown a shoe on the right back hoof. Did you happen to notice the deputy's horse is favoring that leg? They were in the cabin, too, and made a mess. I am so angry. By the way, why did you say I was on the east quarter fence line? You knew where I was."

"Yes, and I also know you well enough to realize this was something serious from the look on your face. I wasn't about to tell them where you really were." He thought for a bit about what she had said. "You know, there could be a lot of horses missing a shoe. Are you absolutely certain about that?"

"Listen, Cal, I'm no expert tracker, but a person doesn't have to be Tonto to see a hoof print that has no shoe. And it was the deepest prints, so I know the rider of that horse was the heaviest in the group, and that so-called deputy is a big guy. By the way, did you happen to notice the way he was undressing me with his eyes? He's no deputy, I'd bet my bottom dollar on it. There's something wrong here, Cal."

Cal took Harmony from Lucy, brushed her down and put her in the pasture. He wasn't too sure what to think about the deputy, but he would take a couple of the guys with him to the cabin tomorrow to check it out and clean it up.

* * *

Sheriff Ganger asked nervously, "Do you think Cal's wife suspected something? She wasn't saying much but wasn't taking her eyes off your horse, either."

"You worry too much, old man. She doesn't know anything. So she likes my horse…so what? Maybe she likes me, too," he laughed.

"I've known Cal Frasier a long time. Can't we use some other ranch? Your grandfather might have been a hard businessman, but he still had some scruples."

Laughing ruthlessly, "Yeah, and you see where those scruples got him. He should have had the Yellow Rose years ago. He was a fool to let Frasier buy it out from under him. We could've all been millionaires by now. He and my dad were both fools. I'm runnin' the show now, and it ain't gonna happen this time. Listen, Sheriff, would you like to retire with money or without? And would you like to stay in one piece or be *accidentally* shot by some rancher? Make your decision now before we get the ball rolling on Cal Frasier's place. I'll take care of his wife."

* * *

As they were eating dinner, Cal told Lucy the man who leased their adjoining ranch had stopped by to let him know he wasn't going to renew his lease.

"After leasing it for so many years, does that seem strange to you, Cal?"

"Maybe a little, but he said he had some health issues. The strange part is that it seems to be a sudden decision, and he said he would be gone in two weeks. That's awfully fast to pack everything up and sell the stock. It does seem strange, but I'll find someone else to lease it."

"Have you thought about combining the two properties and running them both under either the Frasier or Benson name? I'd be happy to look at the numbers for you and do a cost analysis," Lucy offered.

"That would be a big undertaking, Lucy. We would need twice as many hands and new loading chutes and corrals. We'd probably need our own trucks so we could haul the cattle to market ourselves. I'd want to make certain the land was put to good use again."

Lucy smiled as Cal became more enthusiastic about the idea. "So? Are you going to let me run the figures? Then you'll have something concrete to show Ben."

"Sure, go ahead. Look at the costs plus the extra personnel and equipment required. Factor in the cost of hiring another ranch manager. There is a house there specifically for a manager and his family, but it would need some repairs, I'm sure. It hasn't been lived in for years. The main house is in good shape, but I should probably look for a tenant for that. It's not good for a house to sit empty."

Lucy rubbed his shoulders. "This is kind of exciting, isn't it? It would be a huge responsibility for Ben someday, but he'll be able to handle it because he's been taught by the best."

Cal stood up and kissed her. "You flatter me, my dear."

* * *

Cal's daughter, Jackie, called later in the afternoon. "Lucy, would it be possible to have a baby shower for Candy and Ben at the ranch?"

"Oh, that would be so much fun, Jackie. Of course you can. We can have it in the great room where there's plenty of space. That is kind of you to suggest it. I was thinking about the list of things they need for the baby since it is their first one. They literally have nothing. Do you want it to be a surprise or will you tell them?"

"I'm still thinking about that, but I'm afraid it will be hard to make it a surprise since they live there."

"That's true. Well, you have a bit of time to think about it. I will do whatever I can to help. Just don't ask me to bake the cake, okay?" Lucy laughed.

Since she was talking to daughters, Lucy thought she should call her daughter-in-law, Lynne. She hadn't spoken to her for a week or more.

"Lynne, it's good to hear your voice. How are Paul and the kids?"

"The kids are missing you terribly, Lucy. They're having a hard time adjusting to the fact they can't run to your house any time they want. It was nice they could do that when we lived in Batavia."

"Please tell them I miss them, too. Skype isn't quite the same as hugging each other, is it? And we can't bake cookies together on the computer. How is Annie's leg this week?"

"She says it aches if she runs around too much. The doctor told us it will eventually be as good as it was before the accident. I have some news about Paul's job; he's working from home now. He has to attend an all-day meeting once a month, but other than that, all of his work is done here. We had to shuffle things around a bit so he could use a room for his office. We've been looking for a bigger house to rent or buy when the lease is up on this one."

"When does the lease end, Lynne?"

"We signed a year lease, with an agreement we could move at the end of six months if it became necessary. Six months would be August, and a year would be February. Since I continued to homeschool Annie and Jarrod after we moved, it wouldn't affect their school attendance if we found a bigger house in another school district."

"Cal's daughter, Jackie, is planning a baby shower for Ben and Candy. I don't know the date yet, but maybe we could coordinate a visit around the time of the shower. I miss all of you so much."

"We miss you, too, Lucy. I wish Paul and the kids were home, but they went to the grocery for me. I'll tell them you called. Perhaps we can Skype later tonight."

"Yes, let's do that. I'll be waiting to see all of you. Give them hugs for me, Lynne."

CHAPTER 5

AFTER BREAKFAST THE NEXT MORNING, Lucy grabbed her sound-inhibiting earmuffs, as Cal called them, a box of bullets for her revolver, and a bag of cans. She saddled Harmony and made sure she also had her rifle and rope. After her ride the other morning, she wanted to be prepared for whatever or whomever she might encounter.

She led Harmony out of the stable and looked for Cal. She wanted to tell him where she was going.

"This must be some serious riding this morning—saddle and everything," Cal teased as he walked up behind her. Her hair was pulled back in a ponytail, and she had her western hat pulled low on her head. She looked delicious, but he knew she was on a mission, and he wasn't going to try to convince her to come back inside with him.

"I figured we're going to have grandchildren here for possibly the next month, so I wanted to do a little target practicing before I have to lock up my Smith & Wesson. Is it okay with you if I go? I'm going to the bluffs so I have a backdrop for the cans. It's kind of sad that I can't use cans on fence posts anymore, but there's no danger of ricocheting this way."

"It's never all right when you're away from me. I worry about you, Lucy. I can't protect you when you're out there, but I trust you to make good decisions, and I always pray God will bring you back to me, safe and sound. Don't stay out too long, okay?"

"I won't. Before I go, can you adjust these ear protectors so I can hear everything but the explosions of the shots? I never seem to get them on the right setting. I want them as fine-tuned as possible."

Cal fixed the setting, pulled her in to him, tilted her hat back on her head, and kissed her for a long time. He finally let her go. She adjusted her hat, swung up onto Harmony, and rode off toward the bluffs.

Ben walked up as Lucy was leaving. "Why do you let her go, Dad? Aren't you afraid something will happen to her? Maybe you should go with her."

"She needs the time alone, Ben. Lucy was ferociously independent for many years. She handled everything and was proud of the fact she could take care of herself. I know she enjoys feeling safe with me, but I can't smother her. She does everything with a fierceness I can't explain. Whether it's laughing or loving, there is no mediocre in her. It's always all or nothing. I desperately love that about her."

"All I can say, Dad, is she's the best thing that has ever happened to you, and I can only pray Candy and I are still that infatuated with each other when we are your age."

Cal looked at his son, "You will be, Ben, but it takes work. Never forget to tell, and show, Candy how much you love her and want her."

* * *

When she reached her destination, Lucy tethered Harmony in the shade of some tall scrub brush. She placed the cans in the sandy soil of the bluff so they wouldn't tip over. With the sound inhibitors on her ears, she mentally repeated the instructions she learned from her grandpa many years ago. She stood with her feet slightly apart, gripped the handle of her revolver, looked at her target, exhaled, used a smooth and steady trigger pull, and followed through. She hit the first can dead center, then the second, third, fourth, and fifth. She set new cans and reloaded.

She repeated the exercise, but as she was preparing to destroy the third can, she heard the sound of a horse and a man's footsteps quietly approaching from behind. She was sure the person was assuming she could not hear with her ears covered and was planning on getting dangerously close to her. Lucy kept her arm straight out in front of her as she wheeled around. Standing several yards in front of her was Deputy Dawson, leering at her.

"Well, looky there. If it ain't the new Mrs. Frasier. Tell me, Honey, is your husband satisfying you? I bet I could do a better job." He took a step toward her.

"One more step and you will regret it, I promise. I'm going to give you three choices. I can put the first bullet where your fake badge was the other day, or I can take out your gun hand if you even make the slightest move toward that sidearm, or," as she lowered her revolver just a little toward his crotch, "I can make certain you will never think about satisfying a woman again for the rest of your life. Or, if you really want, I can probably make all three happen. If you care to look at those cans back there, you'll see I don't miss, and you will also notice I have only used two bullets which means I have three left…just enough, it seems to me. And if you want references to my ability, I can give you the name of a man in jail in Chicago who will never regain the use of his arm. What do you think?"

She saw him glance at the first five cans on the ground and at the two she had destroyed in the second batch. His face lost some of its bravado. He raised his hands shoulder high and started walking backward.

"Okay, okay, take it easy. I was just playing around. I'm going to get on my horse now, nice and slow. Then I'm going to ride out of here. You wouldn't shoot a man in the back, would you?"

"I don't see a *man* anywhere," Lucy told him. "You're trespassing. Leave this property now, and don't come back."

He rode off, raising a cloud of dust as he went. Lucy slowly brought her arm down. She was trembling, whether from fear or anger, she didn't know. As she watched the dust he was creating grow smaller and smaller in the distance, she told herself, *I should have shot the bastard and let the buzzards pick his bones clean. He isn't going away, I know. He's going to bring big trouble to Cal and this ranch...but not if I can help it.*

On the ride back to the house, Lucy debated about telling Cal what happened. After the last two incidents when she was riding alone, he was sure to tell her she needed to stay close and not go riding by herself anymore. Her main concern was to find out what was going on. This wasn't the sheriff checking on a few stolen cattle; it was much more than that. She was sure of it but couldn't pull all the pieces together yet. She still had a few contacts in Illinois. They might not recognize a cow if they saw one, but they could recommend someone they knew here in Texas. One thing she learned over the years was to make use of her network. It contained a wealth of information and expertise, and she needed to find a trustworthy person to sift through it. There isn't much that can't be learned about a person or company if you have the right hacker on the computer. She smiled. She knew just the person.

* * *

When Lucy rode in, she noticed an unfamiliar car in the drive. She took care of Harmony, grabbed her rifle to lock it up in the house, and walked into the kitchen, carrying the rifle and a box of shells. Cal was sitting at the table drinking coffee with a 30-ish blonde woman who seemed to be hanging on his every word.

Cal stood when Lucy entered the house.

"Lucy, this is Patricia. She heard the other ranch house was going to be empty and wanted to talk about renting it."

"Patricia, this is my wife, Louisa." Cal took the rifle and shells from her. "She doesn't always greet guests with a rifle in her hand."

Lucy extended her hand to Patricia and said, "Hello. I assume you have a large family to fill that big house?"

Patricia smiled and looked at Cal. "No, it's just little ol' me. I want to live where it's peaceful and quiet."

Lucy smiled but was thinking, *Little ol' me…good grief. After the morning I've just had, you could become my second target if you don't stop acting like a heifer in heat when you're looking at my husband.*

Patricia stood and shook hands with Cal. "I should be going. I'm sure I'll see you again, Cal." She touched his arm briefly and smiled up at him as if she knew a secret.

Lucy opened her mouth to make a comment, but thought better of it. Now wasn't the time to act like a jealous teenager. She would discuss this with Cal later.

After Patricia left, Cal asked Lucy, "You missed lunch. Can I fix a sandwich or something?"

"I nearly *was* lunch—for the buzzards. I'm not hungry, but I'll take a glass of sun tea, if there's still some in the refrigerator."

She related the events of her morning. Cal's face darkened as she told him about the deputy. "There's something being planned, Cal, and it won't be good for your cattle business, I guarantee it. Someone is out to destroy you. There are a lot of loose strings floating around. I haven't been able to tie them together yet, but hopefully, with a little help from some old friends, I will find a way."

She could tell by the look on his face, he wasn't buying the whole concept of imminent danger. "I'm going to change clothes. Why don't you see if Ben and Candy can come over this evening, and we can discuss this with them and get their opinion? After all, they certainly have a vested interest in the success or failure of this ranch."

Lucy spent the afternoon looking through her list of trusted contacts, deciding which ones might be the most helpful for what she wanted. She would be asking for a few illegal things, but it didn't matter if it meant protecting Cal. She would fly to Illinois and talk to them in person or find another way to contact them so there would be no trace of calls or texts. The thought of it was exhilarating. She suddenly stopped. *Did that mean she was not content here and was missing the challenges of her old life?* She would definitely have to pray about that.

Chapter 6

"I'LL GRILL A COUPLE OF STEAKS if you want to make baked potatoes and a salad," Cal told Lucy later in the day.

"I can probably handle that," she replied.

Cal didn't know what to do with this quiet, sullen Lucy. She had been working on her laptop all afternoon, barely speaking to him. She didn't even give him a hard time about making fun of her cooking skills. Was she jealous of him talking to Patricia? That seemed impossible. She knew he would never consider looking at another woman. He knew the morning encounter with the deputy had not been good. Maybe she hadn't told him everything that was said.

They ate in relative silence. Lucy only finished half the food on her plate and then pushed it back, saying she wasn't hungry. They loaded the dishwasher and watched the news. It was a welcome relief when Ben and Candy arrived a few hours later.

"What's up, Dad?" Ben asked as he and Candy sat down on the couch closest to the kitchen.

"Some rather strange things have been happening lately, and Lucy thinks they are a vision of things to come concerning the ranch. She believes they are all related, somehow. I don't know that I agree with her, but we do agree that it's only fair to include you and Candy in these discussions. The ranch will be all yours someday, so it only makes sense for you to be involved."

Ben leaned forward. "What kinds of things?"

Lucy took a deep breath, knowing she was probably going to be "spittin' in the wind" because Ben might feel just like Cal did, thinking that she was imagining things.

"When I rode to the cabin, there were tracks everywhere indicating three riders were meeting there for something. The heaviest one rode a horse with a missing shoe on the back right hoof. The same day, the sheriff and his new deputy showed up here. They used the pretense of riding around the ranch looking for signs of stolen cattle. The deputy was on a horse favoring his right back leg. That same person, who I'm certain is not a deputy, tried ambushing me at the bluffs this morning. If I hadn't been able to hear him approaching, he probably would have shot me. Luckily, I still had my gun in my hand. We had a few words, and he apparently felt threatened enough to take my advice and leave. The sheriff has to be involved, also."

Cal interrupted her, "I've known Sheriff Ganger for years. I cannot believe he is involved with any illegal scheme."

Lucy flashed him a look that was not happy. She continued, "If he's not directly involved, he at least knows what's going on. Think about this: the ranger assigned to this county was suddenly transferred, and he's not been replaced. People are meeting for some unknown reason at the cabin. The man who leased your other ranch for 20 years has suddenly decided he wants out of his lease. The deputy was obviously following me. Some crazy woman shows up out of the blue and wants to rent the house on the other ranch. It has over 2,000 square feet of space, but she's all alone. I'm not buying it. Those aren't all coincidences."

Cal was watching her and realized she looked like she was at a board meeting, presenting facts and figures, just like she used to do for her business. Did she miss the challenges of that life? Were he and this ranch life too boring for her? Lately, he found himself asking that question more often. He had always worried just a little that he wouldn't be able to hold onto her forever.

"When you put it all together like that, it does sound feasible, Lucy. But why? Do you have any idea why anyone would be setting these things in place?" Ben asked.

Lucy answered, "Not yet, Ben. But I have some feelers out trying to get an answer or at least a tip on a possible motive." Her phone beeped. She read the message and nodded her head.

Cal was shaking his head. "Are you sure you aren't making a mountain out of a molehill, Lucy? The sheriff is getting ready to retire. Why would he jeopardize his reputation and his pension now? You know, Lucy, you are suspicious of everyone. This isn't Chicago. This is Magnolia, Texas. People here are basically honest and help each other. And, you can't go around threatening to shoot people. The deputy wasn't breaking any laws this morning." Then he added, as an afterthought… "Were you jealous of me talking to Patricia?"

Lucy walked toward Cal until she was only a couple of feet in front of him. She had her hands on her hips and one foot forward a little. Ben remembered his father's words that morning about Lucy's fierceness in everything she did, and he thought he might be about to witness it in action.

Seemingly oblivious to the fact that Candy and Ben were still in the room, Lucy spoke to Cal in a totally "I can't believe you are being so stupid" tone of voice. "Cal Frasier, you are undoubtedly the nicest man I ever met, but please stop being so naïve right now. You're going to have to pull the gloves off and fight for your heritage if you want to keep it. That message I just received told me who the deputy really is. You want to know what's going on? I'll tell you. He's the grandson of Kirk Kitson, the owner of the Double K when you bought this ranch. The old man died, but his son and grandson have a reputation for being the most unscrupulous owners and developers in Texas. They are going to make another run at this ranch and everything you have worked for. My guess is they have a vendetta against you because you outbid them years ago when you bought the Yellow Rose from Leon. You spoiled their plans for a huge sprawling suburban development, and they aren't going to give up until they can make that happen."

Cal looked at Lucy in disbelief. After he let her words sink in for a minute, he had another thought that scared him almost as much. "Lucy, have we just had our first real argument since we got married?"

She responded by saying, "I believe we have." Then she took a step forward, pinning Cal against the wall. She wrapped her arms around his neck and kissed him…hard. When she let her arms drop, she whispered, "That's how I settle an argument."

"I might instigate one every day if that's how we're going to say 'I'm sorry.'"

Lucy retorted, "That's just how I *settle* an argument. If you want an 'I'm sorry' you'll have to come with me to the bedroom."

She left, and Cal suddenly remembered Candy and Ben were still on the couch. He turned and told Ben, "Turn the lights off when you leave."

Candy looked at Ben and burst out laughing. "They are so cute."

Ben helped her up and put his arms around her. "I don't know about cute, but I'm pretty sure I have something to say I'm sorry for. Come on."

They turned the lights off and went to their house.

* * *

Lucy lay snuggled in Cal's arms. "I really am sorry I was so angry with you, Cal. I can't bear the thought of anyone destroying our life here."

"I know. And I'm sorry I didn't trust your instincts. I should have listened. I may know cattle but you know people, and you obviously were right. Now what do we do about it?"

"I'm working on that. But I need some time. Keep your eyes and ears open for anything that seems out of the ordinary and tell the men, too. At least the ones you can trust. It's hard to fight an enemy you can't see coming."

She rolled over and noticed his split lip. "Did I do that to you?"

He licked his lip. Laughing, he told her, "Yes, you did. I wasn't sure when you kissed me if you were loving me or trying to hurt me."

Lucy smiled seductively and said, "Maybe both, Cowboy."

* * *

Several hours later, Lucy was still cradled in Cal's arms, sleeping peacefully. The incessant ringing of her phone finally awakened her. She roused enough to reach for it, but knocked it off the nightstand. *They'll call back,* she thought and snuggled back against Cal.

It did start ringing again. She reluctantly stood up and retrieved it. The message was from Vicki's husband, David. Suddenly Lucy was wide awake. "Cal. Cal...wake up, Honey."

He opened one eye, smiled at her and started to draw her back into bed. She laughed and told him, "No, not now. Vicki's having the baby. I have to go to Cypress to stay with the kids."

"I don't want you to go alone. I'll drive you there, drop you off, and then bring you and the little ones home Sunday after church, okay?"

"You think pretty fast for a man who should be exhausted." She kissed his cheek and headed to the bathroom.

"Do you think you have time for a shower?" he asked.

"Maybe not, but I need one. It will be a five-minute one, I promise. I have an overnight bag packed and ready to go. You can grab it from the closet, and we'll be on our way."

As they sped through the dark countryside in Lucy's car, she was smiling at the thought of a new baby in the family. She wondered how much a baby would upset the apple cart for Bethany and Devon. Even though they knew about the baby, of course, they still had some issues from being in the foster care system for several years. Vicki and David had been warned about feelings of abandonment and had done their best to prepare for those feelings.

She leaned over to Cal. "Do you want to make a wager on whether it's a boy or girl?"

"You're the card shark, Lucy. I would never bet against you."

"Aww, come on. You have a 50-50 chance of being right. How about it?"

He glanced at her and asked, "What do I win if I'm right?"

"A repeat of last night."

"And what do I lose if you're right?"

"I get to go along on the round-up and help bring the calves in."

Cal thought about it for a while. "Why do I get the feeling this is a rigged wager? Do you already know the sex of the baby?"

Lucy feigned indignation. "Why, Mr. Frasier, do you think I would stoop to cheating?"

He smiled and said, "Absolutely, if you thought it would allow you to go on that cattle drive."

They pulled into the Marsh driveway. David was waiting at the door, but went back to get Vicki when he saw the headlights of their car.

"Oh, Mom, I'm so happy to see you. I thought you would never get here."

"Honey, Cal was breaking speed limits all the way."

"I'm sure he was." She glanced at Lucy's wet hair. "Why on earth did you take time to take a shower? It's 3:15 in the morning, for heaven's sake." She paused for a second and glanced at Cal. "Okay, never mind. I don't want to know the answer to that. David will call as soon as we have news."

They left and Lucy looked at Cal. "Aren't adult children fun?" she laughed. "Are you going back now or do you want to stay until David calls? It could be a long time or only a few hours. In my limited experience, babies make their own decisions."

Cal stretched out on the couch and placed his hat over his face. "I'll stay until daylight. If there's no word by then, I'll go back home."

"Before you fall asleep, place your bet. Boy or girl?"

"Mmmm, I'll say a little boy. Okay? I can go to sleep now?"

"Yes, Sweetheart, go to sleep. Sweet dreams. I'm wide awake and hungry. I'm going to find something to eat."

Lucy sat at the kitchen island, eating a roast beef sandwich. "Please, Lord," she said aloud, "keep Victoria safe and let her deliver a healthy baby. They have waited a long time. Thank you for blessing their lives with Bethany and Devon and now, this little one."

It was two hours later when David called. "Louisa, it's a little girl. We got here just in time. Vicki and the baby are fine. I will send a picture to your phone. She's beautiful."

He sent a picture of the baby wearing a pink knitted hat with dark hair peeking out from under it. Her eyes were squinched shut and her hands clenched into fists.

Lucy said a silent prayer. *Thank you, Jesus, for answered prayers. Bless this little one and keep her in your care for her entire life.*

She returned to the living room and watched Cal sleep. She would wake him when the sun came up.

Chapter 7

"PHOEBE? IT'S JERRY. Call me when you have a minute."

Phoebe listened to the message on her phone and then erased it. She wasn't going to call him back, although she wanted to. *Get a grip on your emotions, Phoebe. This will never work, so stop it right now before the feelings get any stronger, and they are definitely getting stronger every time you see him.*

* * *

After breakfast, Lucy drove Vicki's car to take Bethany and Devon to see their new sister. They each had a chance to hold her, although Bethany wasn't too sure about the whole experience. When Lucy held her in her arms, she thought she was the most beautiful baby on the planet. Silently, she prayed, *Jesus, this baby girl needs your loving arms around her in this world. Protect her and bless her life, today and forever.*

"So, does this baby girl have a name yet or is she going to be Baby Girl Marsh forever?" Lucy asked.

David took Vicki's hand and said, "We wanted to honor both grandmothers, so her name is Olivia Rose. Olivia is my mother's middle name and Vicki chose Rose for the Yellow Rose, since it has been a big part of your life, Louisa."

"Do I have permission to cry now or should I wait until I tell Cal?" Lucy asked quietly.

* * *

When Cal came to get Lucy and the children for church on Sunday morning, they struggled with getting the car seats in his truck and fastened correctly.

Lucy was laughing, "Oh my goodness. I never had to do this with my kids. When we got ready to go somewhere, I put them in the back seat and took off. I probably shouldn't tell anyone that. It really dates me, doesn't it? I mean, no seatbelts? Some people think they've been around since…forever."

"See? Another reason I prefer horses. At least when you put a kid on a horse, you don't have to decide which way they should face, forward or backward," Cal observed.

They finally arrived at church with a few books and snacks in hand. Neither one had taken little children to church for a long time. This could be an adventure. Samantha did show up with Amy and Doug. When Ben and Candy came and sat with them, they managed to fill the entire pew. Lucy smiled at Cal over the kids' heads. It felt good to have all of them in church.

Staying at Vicki's house changed the plans to have Samantha and the children for dinner at the ranch. Instead, they treated them at a restaurant in Cypress. Ben and Candy decided to go see the baby while they were in town.

"Ben," Cal advised his son, "make sure you hold Olivia Rose so you get the hang of it before you're holding your own baby in a few months."

"Okay, Dad, I will," he laughed.

Samantha looked tired and sad, Lucy thought. I wish I could talk to her, but I don't think she wants to hear any advice from me.

When they left the restaurant, Cal buckled the children into their car seats while Samantha hung back and walked with Lucy. "Lucy. I know we started out on bad terms but could I please talk to you some time…about Sean and this situation we're in? I know Daddy tried to help, but I need a woman's perspective, and you are the only mother figure in my life."

Lucy tried not to let her surprise show on her face. "Of course, Samantha. Do you want to follow us home today, or would you rather meet somewhere this week? Or I could come to your house after I take the children home later in the week."

"I think I would like to meet you somewhere later in the week. Let me know when you're free."

Lucy impulsively hugged her and whispered, "It will be okay, Honey, one way or the other. God has you in the palm of his hand. Don't forget that."

* * *

Phoebe glanced at her phone. There was another message from Jerry. The man didn't give up easily. How was she supposed to explain a life of disappointments and depression and scars, both imaginary and real? It never mattered before, but now this man had made an inroad into her life and her heart, and she didn't know what to do about it. She supposed she should meet him and tell him she didn't want to see him again instead of ignoring him. He deserved that much.

"Phoebe. It's good to hear your voice. I've been trying to reach you. I thought you fell off the edge of the world or something."

"Hi Jerry. I'm sorry for being evasive. Are you in town?"

"No, not now, but I'm coming to Chicago soon. Can I please see you? I miss you."

She missed him, too. More than she could tell him. She could still taste that first kiss and all the ones after that, too, but she knew where this was going, and it had to stop. Unless there was an entire world power outage with no chance of light anywhere on the planet, she would go to her grave without making love to a man again.

"Call me when you're in town, Jerry. I promise I'll answer my phone, and we can meet and talk, okay?"

* * *

The next day after breakfast, Lucy took Bethany and Devon to the barn to see the horses. She promised a ride on Nell later in the day.

Lucy picked Bethany up so she could see into the stalls. Harmony nibbled a carrot from Bethany's outstretched hand. "That tickles," she giggled.

A young man walked into the barn. He touched the bill of his baseball cap and said, "Good mornin' Ma'am."

Lucy nodded, while scrutinizing him. She didn't know all the men who worked on the ranch, but he didn't look like a cowhand to her. *Don't be shy, Lucy. Just jump right in.* "Who are you and what are you doing here?" she asked, while checking to see where Devon was.

"I'm sorry if I startled you. I just delivered the ATVs your husband ordered a few weeks ago." He motioned to the other barn where he must have unloaded them. "I thought while I was here, I'd come take a look at the horses. Somebody named Ben said it was okay."

Lucy relaxed a little and put Bethany down. "I didn't catch your name," she said.

"Carlos, ma'am." He walked closer and bent down to talk to Bethany, who was hiding behind Lucy's legs. "And who is this pretty little girl?"

"Her name's Bethany, and I'm Devon, her big brother," Devon volunteered before Lucy could stop him.

"Devon, that's a strong name. How old are you, Devon?"

Before Devon could answer, Lucy spoke up. "I think you should probably go back to the barn where you dropped the ATVs, Carlos."

"Sure thing. Sorry I disturbed you. Have a good mornin' Ms. Frasier."

All kinds of warning bells were going off in Lucy's head, but she wasn't sure why. He hadn't really done anything wrong. *Was she overly suspicious of everyone as Cal said?* Maybe, but she couldn't shake the feeling of distrust of Carlos. Was he part of the plan to take the ranch back?

When Lucy checked caller ID, she saw it was Jerry. "Hey Jerry, what's up?"

"I understand you and Cal have a new granddaughter. Tell Vicki and David I said congratulations. Better yet, I will call and tell them."

Lucy thought this was a weird conversation. Did he really call to tell her to convey a message and then decide to do it himself? Jerry continued, "Louisa, I would like you to come to the office the next time you're in town."

"Okay, I can do that. I'm taking the kids home later in the week. Would Wednesday be okay? Around two in the afternoon?"

"Perfect. I'll clear my schedule. See you then."

After Bethany and Devon were tucked in for the night, Lucy told Cal about Jerry's call. "I'm meeting Samantha to talk about her situation with Sean, and I'm sure Jerry wants to discuss Phoebe. I'm either becoming the resident shrink or the biggest busybody in Texas," she observed. "That reminds me, were you in the barn today when the ATVs were delivered?"

"Yep. Ben and I were both there. Why?"

"Did you hear Ben give some young man named Carlos permission to come to the stable to see the horses?"

"No, I don't think so. In fact, we wondered what happened to him after he unloaded them. I take it he was in the stable when you were? Did he do something he shouldn't have?"

"I guess not. He seemed awfully interested in the children instead of the horses. It set off the 'suspicion bells' in my head." She looked at Cal and laughed. "I know, I know. Go ahead and say it." Then she laughed and told him, "Hey, I'm making progress. I didn't threaten to shoot him."

Cal gave her a "thumbs up." "That's a good thing, Lucy." He suddenly had another thought. "I know the baby coming and watching Devon and Bethany has interrupted your days, but have you been able to come up with any figures for working both ranches as one, instead of leasing the Frasier Ranch to someone again?"

"No, I haven't. That's sort of on the back burner for now. I'm much more concerned with getting information on the threat I think is lurking out there. It's like waiting for the other shoe to drop." She continued, "Cal, do you trust your accountant? I mean, implicitly? Hypothetically, if you killed someone, would he help bury the body? That kind of trust, like I trusted Anthony, my project manager in Illinois."

"Yes, I do trust him. I'm certain he would help dig the hole for the body. Why do you ask? Are we going to be burying bodies?"

"I sincerely hope not. But since you trust him and obviously you trust Jerry as your attorney, you need to talk to both of them. They need to be aware of anything suspicious happening with your finances or your legal matters—anything. Honey, I know you still believe I am a little paranoid, but I've had some research done on the Double K operation. They have ties to some extremely dangerous people. They're running the original company as a legitimate development firm, but the grandson has branched out a bit and is capable of anything to get what he wants. He's been investigated for a murder and a few missing people, but no one can prove anything. He's got an uncanny way of covering his tracks. He wants your ranches, and it frightens me. I know it wouldn't ruin you financially, but it would break your heart to see them as housing communities."

"I believe you, Lucy; I just don't understand how he's going to go about getting what he wants. I'm not going to sell willingly, so is he going to come in here with guns blazing and demand the deed?"

"No, it will be more subversive than that. I don't believe he has the brains to blow his nose, but he knows how to get what he wants by bullying and threatening and hiring others to do the work. That's actually true of most 'bad guys' I've ever known. I think I need to make a trip to Chicago. There are some people who may be able to help but they won't want to use the phone or computer to talk to me. It's too dangerous for them. I'm not telling you who they are, either. That way, if you're ever questioned, you can honestly say you know nothing."

"Good God, Lucy. I feel like I'm in the middle of a spy movie. Is it really necessary for you to go? I can't let you go by yourself. The last time you were nearly killed in your office, I got there too late. Let me go with you. You can go to your clandestine meetings, but let me fly with you and be there if you need me."

Lucy smiled at him. "Okay, Cowboy. I would love for you to go along. Can you get tickets for one day next week?"

Chapter 8

SAMANTHA HIRED A SITTER for Amy and Doug while she met Lucy for lunch. They chatted for a bit, until Lucy finally said, "Samantha, it meant a lot to me when you asked to talk to me. I know this can't be easy for you."

Tears immediately rolled down her cheeks and dripped off her chin. "Lucy, I don't know what to do. I never in a million years thought Sean would leave me for another woman."

Lucy handed her some tissues. "Samantha, do you know if Sean is having a physical affair with her or is it an infatuation?"

"He swears he hasn't slept with her, but I don't know if I should believe him or not. I want to, but he has hurt me so much. He told me yesterday he wants to come back home, but honestly, I don't know if I want him to."

"Can you tell me what issues sent him away to begin with? I mean, why did he say he was leaving?"

Samantha managed a slight smile. "Oh, you know…he said I was too bossy and I thought I had to make all the decisions about everything, from big things to little things, and I never had time for him but always had time for my friends and the kids. He felt like I emasculated him, and he wasn't necessary in our lives, so he might as well leave."

Lucy took a deep breath and said a prayer she would say the right thing. "Listen, Samantha, I am definitely not a marriage counselor, and I believe you and Sean need to see one. If you like your pastor or if there is someone he can recommend, that's the first commitment you both need to make. Now, I am going to talk to you exactly like I would talk to my daughter, Victoria, and I can tell you, I am not her favorite person sometimes, but I have to tell you how I feel. Do you think Sean is right about the things he complained about?"

Samantha started crying again. "I've asked myself that question a thousand times. I suppose he is, but I don't know how to stop being in charge. He doesn't want to make any decisions. You can't run a family when no one makes decisions."

"That's true. Believe it or not, you and I are a lot alike. I have a 'git 'er done' personality, while your father likes to think things through. Way too long, sometimes, in my opinion. However, a man needs to feel like a man in a marriage. Don't misunderstand me. I am not saying the husband can run roughshod over his wife and her thoughts and desires. He needs to know how to please her, not just in the bedroom but in little things in everyday life. She needs to know that about him, too. Do you know what television programs Sean likes to watch or where he would like to go if he won a trip or where he would like to retire some day?"

Samantha was staring at her. "No. I never ask anything about his likes or dislikes or his dreams for the future, and our bedroom activities were pretty much non-existent before he left. We didn't take time to talk, we just argued about everything. And we never got over it, because when we argued, one of us would storm out of the room. Can I ask you something? How do you and Dad settle an argument? I mean, you must disagree sometimes, right?"

Lucy hesitated, thinking about their last argument, but decided to plunge ahead. "We have only had one big disagreement, but we settled it by making love all night. It's hard to argue when you can't catch your breath." She looked at Samantha and added, "I know, too much information, right?"

Samantha laughed out loud. "Well, maybe, yes...but I appreciate your honesty and being candid with me." She took a swallow of her soda and seemed to be considering the things Lucy told her. "When Sean calls tonight, I'll ask him if he's willing to go to counseling. That will be the first step. Maybe there's hope for our marriage."

"Don't forget to pray about it, Samantha. Praying as a couple is so important. I would never have believed that before I met your father. He's taught me many things, and I thank God every day for him."

As they were leaving, Samantha hugged Lucy for a long time. "You are a special person, Lucy, and I will remember to thank God for putting you in my dad's life."

* * *

Lucy drove to Jerry's office to see what the next problem was. Jerry extended his hand, but she hugged him instead. "Are you ready to call me Lucy yet, or are you still stuck on Louisa?"

Jerry smiled. "I like the sound of Louisa, and besides, it makes our friendship special if everyone else calls you Lucy."

"You know, Vicki's husband, David, always calls me Louisa. All these years, and he never calls me Lucy. I'll ask him about that sometime. But you didn't ask me to come here to talk about Vicki and David."

Jerry frowned. "Actually, I did. I'm probably breaching all kinds of protocol by talking to you about this, but I can't talk to them just yet. I mean, they brought a new baby home just a few days ago. I desperately need your advice."

"Okay, Jerry, now you're frightening me. What is it?"

He reached into a desk drawer and pulled out some papers. "I received these last week from the agency that handled the adoption. Apparently, the state of Texas did not practice due diligence when trying to locate the unnamed father of Bethany and Devon. He has surfaced and is claiming legal custody of his children."

Lucy didn't know whether to cry or have a tantrum. She decided on the latter. "How the hell could this happen?" she yelled at Jerry. She stood up and began pacing the room. "He can't just show up and expect to get his children back. I doubt he even knew he had children until a few months ago."

She leaned over his desk, dark eyes flashing, and asked, "Exactly what are you going to do about this mess?"

Jerry knew when he made the decision to tell Louisa, he was going to feel the brunt of her fury. After she calmed down a bit, he managed to tell her a few things. "He isn't going to be handed the children just because he showed up. There will be a review of negligence on the state's part, he will be subject to a paternity test to determine if he is the biological father, and then he will have to prove he can provide for them if he would be granted custody. My biggest concern right now is keeping them safe. He doesn't exactly have a stellar background, which is a good thing if we want to prove he wouldn't be fit to have them. But it could be a bad thing if he would decide to snatch them and run."

Lucy sat down and leaned her head on the back of the chair. *Dear God, can there be one more thing to add to my life right now? I am handing everything back to you. Please help me keep all these things in perspective.*

She heaved a deep sigh. "Okay, Jerry. What do you want me to do? Cal says I have to stop threatening to shoot people, so I hope you have an alternative plan in mind."

"I thought perhaps you could offer to take the children to the ranch for a while. Maybe tell Vicki you want to give her some time to bond with the baby or something. They would be safe with you and Cal. No one has you associated with the Marsh name, if someone was looking for them."

"You underestimate the information that can be obtained if someone wants it badly enough, my friend. Cal is getting tickets for us to fly to Chicago on some ranch business. David's company has granted him paternity leave, so Vicki and David will have to be told. They can keep the kids safe until we get back. Let me guess. You want me to tell them, right?"

Jerry nodded. "I would appreciate it very much." He hesitated for a few seconds and then continued, "Now I have another matter to discuss with you."

Lucy was sure this day was never going to end. "Shoot. It can't be any worse than what you just told me."

"How long have you known Phoebe? I assume she has told you we are seeing each other."

Lucy nodded. "Yes, she did tell me. We've known each other since she and her husband moved to Illinois a couple of years after John and I did. They lived a few doors down from our first little house. Our kids played together. Why?"

Jerry looked confused. "She told me she didn't have any children, just like me."

Lucy wanted to kick herself. *Dammit. Now where was she going to go with this?*

"She was married once upon a time Jerry, and she did have a son. I can't tell you more than that. She is going to kill me for telling you that much."

"Louisa, please. I really care for Phoebe, but she has some issues that stop her from confiding in me or even telling me how she feels about me. I think she feels the same as I do, but we don't seem to be making any progress."

"I'll make time to see her when we go to Illinois. I'll talk to her and try to talk some sense into her head, but she's probably the most stubborn person I know, even worse than me. Let me ask you something. When you say you care for her, what does that mean? Do you love her? Do you want to marry her? Do you want to spend the rest of your life with her? Would you be willing to accept her no matter what you discovered about her?"

Jerry was considering answers to Lucy's fast and furious questions which were hitting him like darts thrown at a dartboard.

"I do love her. I would like to marry her and make both our lives complete. I believe she loves me too, but if we even begin to be intimate, and by that I mean a few passionate kisses, she pulls away like she is scared to death. I don't know what to do about that."

Lucy looked at this tormented man and made a decision she was probably going to regret. "Okay, Jerry. I will lose a very valuable friendship over this, but if it helps you and Phoebe have even a glimmer of happiness, it will be worth it."

"Phoebe's husband was an extremely abusive man. They had a sweet little boy named Todd. When her husband would start beating on her, Phoebe always made sure she protected Todd. She was afraid to take Todd and leave because her husband threatened to harm him, knowing he was Phoebe's life. She didn't have any family she could go to for help. When Todd was about 8 years old, his father fell asleep with a burning cigarette. The little house was engulfed in flames. Her husband died in the fire. Phoebe tried to save Todd, and she did get him out of the house, but he died a week later in the hospital. Phoebe's torso was burned so badly that she wasn't expected to live. When she could finally be told that Todd died, she didn't *want* to live. She gave up, blamed God, and begged for someone to end her life. I stayed with her as much as I could. Burns are horrible things; the skin grafting and the scraping of old tissue makes me nauseous even now. She spent nearly a year in the hospital. When she finally was released, she not only had mental and emotional scars, she had physical ones. Her body's reflection in the mirror was an everyday reminder of what she lost. With years of therapy, she recovered and is the Phoebe we know today, but she will never let you see her physical scars. That's what you are battling, my friend."

Jerry had tears in his eyes. "That would never matter to me, Louisa. How can I convince her of that if she won't share her story with me and I can't tell her I know?"

"I really don't have the answer, Jerry. Pray about it, every day and every hour. Get on your knees and ask God to show you a way. I am fresh out of answers for today."

Chapter 9

LUCY WANTED DESPERATELY to go home, but she knew she had to stop and talk to David and Vicki before she left Cypress. They needed to know, but she had no idea how to tell them. She decided to stop at church and take a mental break before going to their house.

The church was quiet and semi-dark inside. Lucy sat down in a pew and closed her eyes. *Heavenly Father, you have heard all my conversations today. Guide my words and help me say the right things to David and Victoria. They are so grateful for their family; please don't allow their world to unravel. Keep them and the children safe, now and after we get them to the ranch. Please don't let the father take them away. Be with me when I speak to Phoebe, too. She is going to feel so betrayed and has every right to feel that way. Put your hand on Samantha and Sean and their marriage, and please let me help Cal save his land and his heritage. Show me who can help with information. I feel helpless, but I know all things are possible with you. Thank you for your continued blessings.*

Pastor Kelly had entered the sanctuary while Lucy was praying. When she opened her eyes, he asked if he could sit down beside her. "Are you okay, Lucy?" he asked.

"I feel better now that I've talked a few things over with God," she answered.

He nodded and smiled. "Yes, I always feel that way, too, although many times I do all the talking and don't wait in silence to hear what God might have to say to me. All too often, we assume prayer is a one-way conversation."

"You're absolutely right, Pastor. I ask for God's guidance but then immediately charge off to fix things my way. Perhaps I'll sit here a little longer and be silent to hear God's thoughts about my problems."

"If you ever need to talk, Lucy, I'm always available. Would you like me to pray with you now?"

She nodded, and they prayed together for peace and insight in any situation that occurred. Lucy left the church feeling much better equipped to speak to David and Victoria.

* * *

Devon answered the door when Lucy rang the doorbell. She made a mental note to tell David not to let him do that in the next few days or weeks. "Hi, Gramma," he said with a big grin. He was off to the kitchen, yelling, "Mom, Dad, Gramma Lucy is here."

David met her in the hallway and gave her a kiss on the cheek. "Hi Louisa. Nice to see you."

Vicki was holding Olivia when Lucy finally reached the kitchen. "May I hold her?" Lucy asked. Vicki handed Olivia to her. Lucy sat in the family room on the couch with Devon on one side of her. "So, Devon, how are you doing at being a big brother?"

His ear-to-ear grin said it all. "I like it. I get things for Mommy and sometimes I hold Olivia while I sit in the rocker. You have to keep your hand behind her head, y'know."

"Yes, I do know that, but thank you for reminding me. Where's Bethany?" Lucy asked, knowing she would be on the other side of her if she knew Lucy was there.

"She's napping for a bit before dinner," Vicki said. "Actually, she was sent to her room for a time-out, and she fell asleep while she was there."

There was no easy way to tell them so she took a deep breath and asked if she could speak to them alone.

While Devon was concentrating on a new movie, Lucy told them everything Jerry had told her. Vicki's face turned white, and David had to catch her before she fell. They were angry, frustrated, unbelieving, and scared to death.

"So what do we do? Lock them in a closet until this is over?" David said under his breath so Devon wouldn't hear.

"I know it's a nightmare. Cal and I have to go to Chicago in the next couple of days, but as soon as we return, we can take them to the ranch until this is settled. They will be safe there."

"That's impossible," Vicki said quietly. "These things could take a year or more. Are we supposed to have our children living somewhere else for a year? No. We will keep them safe right here. This is their home. Bethany already has some problems related to adoption. Moving her would only exacerbate those feelings of abandonment. I won't do that to them."

David agreed. "We need to be responsible for their safety, not you and Cal. If they had to live with someone, you two would be our first choice, but we will handle this."

Lucy suggested they allow Bethany and Devon to come for a visit while they implemented the safety measures they were talking about installing at their home. She suddenly had a thought. "I know someone who is the best at high-tech security systems. Not your ordinary security, but a system that would record every tiny movement anywhere on the property or in the house. Do you want me to call him and see if he would consider coming out of retirement for one job?"

Vicki and David looked at each other and nodded. "Yes, of course. Anything that might help. Do you have any idea of the cost for that kind of system? Not that it matters when it comes to the safety of the children," David said.

"Don't worry about cost. There won't be any. This is a job between old friends. That's how we work."

Lucy reluctantly handed Olivia Rose back to Vicki. She hugged Devon and told him to give Bethany a hug from her when she woke up. As David walked her to her car, she remembered she wanted to ask him something. "David, just out of curiosity, why do you never call me Lucy? I don't mind you calling me Louisa; in fact I like it, but I was wondering why."

He smiled at her. "The first time I met you, when I started dating Vicki, you were intimidating to me. My image of you as the wickedly powerful business woman who could accomplish anything and had connections everywhere has never faded, I guess. I still see you as Louisa."

"That's perfectly okay with me, David. As long as you know that description doesn't fit me any longer."

As he watched her drive away, he smiled and said aloud, "Yeah, right, Louisa. That description still fits. Who else knows someone who will come from *who knows where* and install a high-tech security system and not charge anything?" He shook his head in amazement.

* * *

As Cal was coming in from the barn, he met Lucy in the drive. She had fast-food containers in her hand. Cal knew it must have been a long day because she rarely ate fast food. He took the bags from her, put the contents on paper plates, and waited for her to tell him what happened.

She took a swallow of her iced tea and sighed. "Cal, I don't even know where to start. The good news is Samantha and I had a very interesting conversation. She is going to pursue marriage counseling if Sean will agree. That's the last good part of my day. Oh wait, I did get to hold Olivia Rose—that was good too."

Cal waited, not sure if he wanted to know the rest of the day's adventures.

"I met with Jerry. It seems the state was negligent in their efforts to find the biological father of Bethany and Devon, and now he has come forward and wants his children. Jerry wanted me to break that news to David and Vicki. Then he also wanted information about Phoebe. He loves her and wants to make a life together, but she is too hesitant and I seem to be the only person on earth who knows why. So…I took the chance of losing my best friend and her trust and told him the whole story of Phoebe's life. I stopped at church and prayed before going to Vicki's. Then I proceeded to tell them they could lose their children. I am exhausted and tired of acting like I know what I'm doing, and I think I'm going to go cry now."

She stood up and started for the bedroom. Cal caught her arm and pulled her over to the couch. He wrapped her in his arms and let her cry until she fell asleep on his chest. He brushed her dark hair off her forehead and thought for the thousandth time since he first met her, how much he loved her. Could he keep her safe? A small part of her still had connections in the dangerous world he thought he had rescued her from. She was willing to step back into that world and risk her life, probably, to save him and the land he loved. Had he paid enough attention to what she was telling him about the day the deputy followed her? She said he undressed her with his eyes in the drive that first day, but he must have made advances or threats toward her when she threatened to shoot him. He chastised himself for not asking for more details. Of course, the deputy had probably made advances or worse. Cal vowed he would kill him if he ever threatened her again or laid a hand on her.

Lucy stirred but didn't wake up. He picked her up and carried her to the bedroom. He removed her shoes, left her in her clothes and pulled the covers over her. He lay down next to her, on top of the covers, just as he had the night after she shot Derek, the man who held her hostage in her office. He could honestly say his life was never boring since he met Lucy.

Chapter 10

SOMETIME IN THE MIDDLE OF THE NIGHT, Lucy threw the covers back and sat straight up in bed. Cal nearly rolled off the other side.

"What is it, Lucy?" he asked groggily.

"I know who Carlos was. He wasn't here to check out your ranching operation or the horses; he was here to see Bethany and Devon. He's the man claiming to be their father."

She dropped back onto the pillow. "So much for Jerry's theory about him never finding them here. He had to get that information from the adoption agency somehow because that's the only place my name is associated with Vicki and David's."

"Go back to sleep, Sweetheart. There's nothing you can do about it at 4 in the morning. As you like to tell me, at least now you have a face for your enemy, right?"

"Mmmm, I guess you're right. By the way, how did I get in bed? The last thing I remember was falling asleep on your chest."

Cal smiled at her. "I carried you in here. I wanted you to be comfortable."

"Wow. You must have eaten your Wheaties yesterday, or you've been working out." She got out of bed. "I'm going to get into my pajamas."

When she came back to bed, she looked at Cal. "Come on, Hercules, get under the covers and put your arm around me. We can still get a few hours of sleep before the sun comes up."

* * *

"Candy, I made you some breakfast. Do you want me to bring it in there or do you want to eat out here?" Ben asked.

Candy came to the kitchen table, slowly. "Oh Honey, you didn't have to do that. I would have had a bowl of cereal or something."

"I know, but I wanted to do it for you. I like to start my day looking at you across the table." Candy smiled at this man who was so good to her. "I heard from Mom yesterday. She wants to come when the baby is born. I don't know if I want her here or not."

Ben tilted his head to one side. "There's plenty of room if that's what you're worried about. Did she indicate how long she would stay?"

"It's not the room. You know we aren't very close. I don't have anything to say to her. I've known Lucy less than a year, and I feel like she's my mother figure."

"I don't know what to tell you. I guess it's up to you. I don't want her being here to upset you and cause problems. Will your dad want to come, too?"

Candy's face turned white. "Oh my stars, I hope not. The two of them here together would make me go into labor for sure. No…no, that can't happen. They act like two spoiled brats when they're together. We would have three babies…them and our newborn."

Ben chuckled at the picture he had in his mind. "What can you do? You can't tell her she isn't welcome."

"Sure, I can. She never had any trouble telling me what she thought of me all the years I lived at home. Neither one of them had time to come to our wedding, so they don't need to come for our baby, either. This baby will have Cal and Lucy for grandparents. That's all it needs."

* * *

Lucy checked the time in Florida and dialed Anthony's number. He answered on the first ring. "Hey Anthony, how are you and Emma? I thought you might be out on the beach already this morning. This is Louisa."

"I know who it is, Honey. No beach this morning, it's raining. Emma and I were just trying to decide if we wanted to crawl back under the covers and listen to the rain, y'know?"

Lucy smiled to herself. "Yes, Anthony, I do know. I wish we had some of that rain. It's the third day of a small heat wave here and very dry."

"I know you didn't call to talk about the weather. What can I do for you, Louisa?"

After she asked if he was still involved in the security business, Lucy briefly explained the circumstances. She told him it was a five-bedroom house situated on a fairly large property. Anthony asked a few more questions. "I would do anything for you, Louisa, but let me talk it over with Emma, okay? I'll call back within an hour."

"Anthony, if you decide to come, I'll buy your tickets and make sure you have a rental car and a hotel close to their house. You would be more than welcome to stay here, but I thought you would like to be closer to your work. I'll wait to hear from you."

Lucy mentally checked that off her list. Now to call Jerry. She dialed his number; his secretary said he was preparing to leave for court. "I hate to do this but can you please ask if he has a few minutes? It's very important."

Jerry picked up. "Louisa? What is it?"

"I've seen the kids' father. I'm certain he was here delivering some ATVs Cal and Ben bought. He said his name was Carlos. If I'm right, he definitely knows where we live and where the children might be part of the time. I've contacted an old friend in Florida who, hopefully, is coming to install a high-tech security system at David and Vicki's house. Someone at the adoption agency, perhaps inadvertently, must have given him my information."

"Are you sure this was the father? I mean, did he tell you that?"

Lucy rolled her eyes, even though Jerry couldn't see her. "No, he didn't tell me that. But I am 99 percent sure it was him. Just wanted you to know, and I apologize for delaying your departure for court. Maybe we'll see you in Chicago tomorrow."

* * *

Anthony called back. "Emma says she would love a vacation in Texas. When do you need the job done?"

Lucy shook her head. "I'm sorry to say, I need it yesterday, Anthony. Tell me when you can leave, and I'll send the money for your tickets. It's easier if you make the purchase."

"I need to contact the main warehouse and have them ship the materials to your daughter's house. This could get expensive, Louisa."

"Not nearly as expensive as losing my two grandchildren. There will be compensation for your time, too, Anthony."

He laughed. "No, ma'am. You prepaid for anything I could ever do for you the day I retired. I will call back one more time about the arrival dates, after I know when the supplies will be there."

Lucy smiled. One of the last things she did when she closed her business accounts was to make sure Anthony and his beloved Emma would have a nice retirement.

* * *

When they were on the plane, Cal asked, "Did you call Phoebe and tell her we were coming?"

Lucy shook her head. "No, I didn't. I was afraid Jerry might have already told her that I shared her life's secrets with him. Then she would refuse to see me, and I really want to talk to her about those secrets and her involvement with Jerry. Did he tell you when his flight was scheduled to arrive?"

"Some time later in the day, I believe."

Cal had reserved rooms in one of the nicest hotels in downtown Chicago. It had great views of the city, an Olympic-sized pool, hot tubs in the rooms, and a five-star restaurant. After they were settled in their room, Lucy asked Cal, "Did you remember to pack your shorts or swim trunks? We're going for a walk along one of the beaches at Lake Michigan, and even though it's one of the less crowded ones, you might draw a bit of attention to yourself if you're wearing cowboy boots and jeans, my dear."

Cal reached into his bag, pulled out a pair of cut-off shorts and held them up. "See? I always do what my wife tells me."

"Yeah, right," Lucy laughed. She changed into a swim suit and a cover-up and stuffed two beach towels into a bag. "Let's find a cab and go to the beach."

They sat on their towels, enjoying the sunshine and the cool breeze. There weren't many people around this early in the day. "We need to look like typical sunbathers, Honey. Why don't you take your t-shirt off so I can put sunscreen on your back?" Lucy was always amazed at Cal's broad shoulders. "You are just one hunk of a man, Cowboy," she told him as she slathered the cream on his back.

Cal laughed at her. "Lucy, can you tell me what we're doing here? I'm pretty sure we didn't fly all the way to Chicago so you could tell me you like my shoulders."

"This beach is a good place to receive a phone call without the signal being traced to a particular tower. Don't ask me why, I just know it is. I learned that a long time ago. The person who is getting the information I want needs to be protected and untraceable phone calls are required."

They drank their bottled waters and talked, pretending to be ordinary beach bums on a beautiful day. Cal saw Lucy answer a phone call. The phone must have been set on vibrate because he never heard it ring, and he was certain he had never seen that phone before. Lucy said nothing, only listened, and then ended the call.

"Have you had enough sunbathing?" she asked him. "Let's go for a walk along the beach."

They picked up the towels and sunscreen and walked farther along the shore. When they reached a desolate area, Lucy threw the phone into a trash bin. "It's untraceable," she explained. "It's a burner phone."

Cal shook his head; he was definitely out of his element. "Can you tell me what you know now that you didn't know when we left home?"

"Yes. The Double K is still being run by the son of the original owner, but the grandson...oh, he is a piece of work. He's in debt to the syndicate. They probably don't want your ranch, but they will want him to pay up. The only way he can do that is to have the deeds to any land that would be good for development. His organization is called Carmion. The emails sent and received indicate the plan is modern-day rustling, on a mega scale. They will probably start with a few head to make owners believe it is somebody needing some fast cash. When the rancher's guard is down, they will bring in the semis, the GPS tracking systems, all high-tech equipment. Anyone who gets in the way will have to be dealt with. He knows a rancher can absorb some losses, but he intends to take entire herds. He's obviously pretty desperate, and desperate men make stupid mistakes. That's a good thing for us."

"How can he possibly hope to move that many cattle so fast? I suppose if he hires enough bull haulers, he can do it. He'll pack them in like sardines," Cal was thinking out loud. "Seems like it would make more sense to poison the water supply."

"Except you forget, he needs all the cash he can get. Dead cows aren't worth anything. Not only does he want to make you desperate enough to sell, he wants the money from the sale of the cattle, too. Plus, herds of dead cattle would definitely be evidence of foul play. Missing herds leave no evidence; it's the rancher's word about how many head were taken."

CHAPTER 11

WHEN THEY RETURNED to the hotel, Cal suggested they go swimming in the indoor pool since they were already in their swim suits.

"If I start to drown, you'll save me, right?" she asked him.

"Aren't you a strong swimmer? That surprises me for some reason."

"I am a strong swimmer, but I might need saving anyway. You can give me mouth-to- mouth resuscitation."

"We don't have to bother going to the pool for me to do that," he laughed.

She pretended to snap him with her towel as they left for the pool.

"What else is on your agenda for today?" Cal asked as they floated in the warm water after swimming a few laps.

"I have to see someone in the downtown area, but I couldn't go there this morning. You can come along and have coffee while you wait for me, but I will have to go to the meeting alone. That's the only way I can get what I want. Then you can go with me to the State Attorney's office. I also want to see Phoebe today after she gets home from work. I guess that's it."

"Would you like to go out tonight? Dinner and dancing, maybe?"

"Ohhh, I would love to, but I didn't bring any clothes for that kind of evening."

"Then save a little time when we're downtown, and you can pick something out."

"Honey, you never tell a woman who is shopping for a new dress that she has a *little* time to find the perfect one," Lucy chuckled.

As they climbed out of the pool, Cal told her, "Lucy, you could wear a gunny sack as far as I'm concerned and still look beautiful, but I want this to be a special night."

* * *

They returned to the room and ordered a light lunch from room service. Then it was time to call a cab to go downtown to the heart of the city. Cal took a seat at a small delicatessen where he could watch the front of the building Lucy was entering across the street. He didn't like this feeling of helplessness at all, but she insisted she would be back in 30 minutes. If she wasn't, he was going in after her.

Lucy entered the small Italian restaurant and quietly told the waiter she had an appointment to see Roberto. He checked the contents of her purse and told her to go to the back. When she entered the inner sanctum, as Roberto liked to call his office, she was lightly patted down for a weapon. Finding none, she was escorted through another door.

"Louisa. You look beautiful as always, my dear," Roberto said as he hugged her. "To what do I owe this honor? I heard you left the Windy City."

"You heard correctly. I'm only here on business, and I need your help."

He gave her a sleazy smile. "I always knew the day would come when Louisa would need me."

"Don't get too excited, Roberto. I don't need *you* exactly. I need information you may have."

He leaned forward in his chair and asked, "Why should I give you any information? You nearly had me sent to prison for 20 years."

"Yes, but obviously you managed to weasel your way out of it, because here you are."

He grinned. "You know, I always liked you, Louisa. You had more balls than any man I ever knew."

Louisa raised an eyebrow. "I'll take that as a compliment…I think."

"I heard you shot Derek with that nice little revolver you always carried." He was looking at her purse as he said it.

Lucy raised her hands slightly. "Hey, your associates already searched my purse and patted me down. No firearms with me today, okay?"

He tried to decide if he believed her or not. "Okay. What do you want to know?"

"I want information on an organization called Carmion. I already know who is running it; I want to know how big the operation is and who is financing it. I also want to know if a woman named Patricia is involved in any way."

Roberto chewed on his cigar for a minute, assessing her. "And what, exactly, do I get out of this transaction, Louisa?"

She leaned on his desk, grabbed the cigar out of his mouth, ground it out in the ashtray and whispered, "When I meet with the State Attorney later this morning, I won't tell him the names of your three boys who are running drugs at the Cook County Jail."

Roberto paled a bit and tried to decide if she was bluffing. Finally, he motioned for one of the men in the room to get her the printout of the information she asked for.

Lucy checked the papers she was handed, and when she was satisfied, she put them in her bag.

"You know, Louisa, you don't have to hurry off. We could have a drink or two and a nice game of poker while you're here."

She smiled at him. "Don't be foolish, Roberto. I don't have time, and besides, we both know who would win, right?"

He nodded his head. "Yes, I suppose so."

Lucy walked out into the sunshine and joined Cal for a coffee. She checked her phone. "Did I make it in 30 minutes?"

"Yes, but it was the longest 30 minutes of my life, Lucy. I know I told you not to threaten people with your gun any more, but did you really go in there without it?"

She smiled coyly at him. "There are some places a lady can carry a smaller firearm and a quick pat-down won't find it."

They walked to the building that housed many government offices. When they reached the third floor, they were ushered into the office of the State Attorney. Lucy introduced Cal to Jason Clifford, a man she had known for many years and someone she trusted implicitly. She asked if he could suggest someone in the Texas office that was just as honest and trustworthy. After explaining what they suspected was going to happen at the ranch, he gave them the name of a man who could help them.

"Okay, now we get to go shopping. Woo-hoo." Lucy was grinning at him.

* * *

By the time she found the dress and shoes she wanted and Cal had purchased slacks and a jacket, it was time to go to Phoebe's house.

When she knocked on the door, she felt more uneasy than she was in Roberto's office.

Phoebe opened it and squealed in delight. "Lucy…Cal. Wow. What are you guys doing here? Come in, come in. You didn't tell me you were coming; I would have made dinner."

Lucy hugged her friend. "It's okay. Cal is taking me out for a special evening." She held up her bags. "I even have a new dress and shoes."

"Well, what are you doing in town? Oh wait, I remember—you said something about business when we talked, right?"

"Yes, but business is done. Now I want to talk to you, Phoebe."

"This sounds serious." She grinned at Cal. "Should I pour a glass of wine before we talk?"

Cal told her he was going to the kitchen to find a glass of water. He would leave them alone to discuss whatever it was that needed to be discussed.

Lucy looked at him and mouthed the word, "coward" when Phoebe didn't see her.

"Okay, my friend, what's up?" Phoebe asked.

"I don't know how to say this exactly, so I'll jump right in. I was in Jerry's office last week because he had some more adoption papers for me to look at. Then he asked me about you, Phoebe, and why you always pull back when he gets a bit serious."

Phoebe had stopped smiling. "And what exactly did you tell him, Lucy?"

"I tried hedging, but he was so miserable and tormented about the whole thing, so at the risk of losing my best friend, I told him everything."

Phoebe's mouth dropped open, and her eyes were huge. "You did not. Tell me you didn't, Lucy. How dare you? What gives you the right to tell my personal secrets to someone? You're right about one thing; you ruined our friendship forever. You can leave now. Get out of my house."

Lucy grabbed her shoulders and shook her. Phoebe was hysterical, and Lucy felt like slapping her just to get her attention, like they did in the movies.

"Phoebe, stop it. Do you hear me? You can hate me forever, but right now I want you to listen to me. Jerry loves you. He told me so. He wants to make a life with you. He won't care about anything but loving you, if you let him. Don't shut him out."

"He may say that now, but he will care, I guarantee it. No man wants a woman who looks like a freak," she sobbed.

Lucy took her hand and led her to the bedroom. "Undress, Phoebe. Take your clothes off. Now."

Phoebe was crying so hard she was having trouble taking her shirt off. "Why? What for?"

Lucy handed her a robe. "Put it on but don't button it. Now turn around and look in the mirror."

"I can't. I just can't."

Lucy grabbed her and gently turned her around. "Look, Phoebe. Look at your reflection. What do you see?"

"I see a woman with big scars from her chest to her legs."

Lucy forced her head up to look straight into the mirror. "Look at this part of you. What do you see?"

"I don't know."

"I will tell you what I see. I see a beautiful woman with luminous eyes, clear skin, thick brown hair, and a smile that would charm the socks off someone. Please don't do this to yourself, Phoebe. Jerry loves you. He will see the same things I did. The scars don't matter. Surely it is worth taking the chance to find out, isn't it? If he turns away from you, you don't want him anyway. If he accepts you as you are, you can have a beautiful life together. We all have scars of one kind or another. Yours may be more obvious, but so what? That's what makes you who you are. You can't change it. What is the alternative? Spend the rest of your life alone and become a bitter old crone? You have way too much going for you to let that happen, my friend."

Phoebe had stopped crying and was sniffling. "I don't think I can do it, Lucy. I don't think I can show Jerry what I look like." The doorbell rang. "That's him now. We were going to talk tonight, and I was going to tell him I couldn't see him anymore."

Lucy buttoned a few buttons on Phoebe's robe. "Okay, now listen to me. This is what we're going to do. I am going out there and tell Jerry to come into your bedroom. You are going to unbutton your robe and show him your scars." Phoebe was shaking her head. "Yes, you are. It's better to do it all at one time; like ripping a bandage off." She put her arms around her friend. "Cal and I will stay in the living room. If Jerry leaves, I will come in and let you cry your heart out on my shoulder. If he chooses to stay, we will tiptoe out and lock the door behind us. Deal?"

Phoebe nodded slowly. "I guess. Will you pray for me? I am scared to death."

Lucy nodded, thinking she had never heard Phoebe talk about prayer in any way. She turned the lights down until it was as dim as candlelight in the room.

When she walked out to the living room, Cal and Jerry were talking. "Jerry, Phoebe is waiting to talk to you in her bedroom." She gave him a look that said, *"You better not screw this up."*

She patted the cushion next to her on the couch after Jerry closed the bedroom door. "Come sit for a minute, Honey. I told her we would stay for a bit to see if she needed us. Otherwise, we would leave and close the door behind us."

When she and Cal left a few minutes later, he asked, "I know they aren't teenagers, but are we promoting pre-marital sex?"

"Maybe, but I don't really think that's going to happen tonight. I think they're going to discover all kinds of things about each other and about themselves, but not necessarily be totally intimate until they're married. Phoebe is too unsure of herself, and Jerry's faith and his moral compass will keep him from consummating that relationship until they do get married."

She stopped walking and turned to him. "Of course, I could be totally wrong, too. I remember wanting you so badly before we were married, I couldn't stand it. It's a good thing you had some self-control, because I didn't."

Cal kissed her when they were in the cab. Then he whispered in her ear, "I have news for you. I have absolutely no self-control when it comes to you, Lucy Mae."

Chapter 12

JERRY TURNED THE HANDLE to Phoebe's bedroom door with much trepidation. When he arrived at her house, he hadn't been prepared for Lucy and Cal to be there or for Lucy to direct him to Phoebe's bedroom. He took a deep breath and walked in. The lights were turned low and Phoebe was sitting on the side of the bed, dressed in her robe.

She looked as though she had been crying for a while, although she was quiet and unsmiling at the moment. He walked to her and held out his hand. She placed hers in his and stood. He pulled her to him and put his arms around her. He whispered in her ear, "Why were you crying, Phoebe?"

"I'm afraid, Jerry."

"Afraid of what? Lucy told me your story. Did you really think I would care about any of that?"

"I didn't want to find out if it would matter or not. If I told you I didn't want to see you again, it would be over, and I wouldn't have to think about it any longer. But I didn't really want it to be over."

Jerry unbuttoned her robe. He traced a finger along one of her scar lines. "I think you're beautiful, Phoebe, and I would like to spend the rest of my life convincing you to see yourself that way."

* * *

When Cal and Lucy finally returned to their hotel room, they made the decision to have dinner in one of the hotel dining rooms instead of the restaurant they had chosen earlier. There was a dance floor, and tonight there would be a band instead of a DJ, so it was easier than going out again.

Lucy came out of the bedroom wearing her new dress and carrying her shoes. The dress was form-fitting down to the waist with a knee-length filmy, swishy skirt. Cal looked at her and commented, "I'm pretty sure you couldn't hide a weapon in there no matter how small it was." She laughed at him and sat in the chair to buckle the straps on her high-heeled shoes. Cal knelt in front of her and buckled them for her.

"You look fantastic, Honey. I don't want to leave this room," Cal told her.

"I don't want to go, either. But you said earlier you wanted to go dancing, so let's go dance a few dances, and then we can come back and order room service, if we want to," Lucy suggested.

They took the elevator to the main floor. There weren't many people in the dining room, but the band was quite good. They ordered a bottle of wine with dinner, since they had changed plans again and decided to eat there, after all.

"Lucy, do you have any idea how much I love you?" Cal asked her.

"Yes, I think I do, and I don't ever want to be away from you, Cal. What I said on our wedding day is still true. You complete me in every way."

They enjoyed several dances. When the music was a slow tune, they held each other tightly and swayed to the music, with Lucy resting her head on Cal's chest. Even with heels on, she didn't begin to reach his height.

Cal spoke to the lead man in the band, requesting a song. Then he borrowed a guitar from one of the band members and played it while he sang, "I Want to Be Your Man" to her.

The lyrics fit the occasion perfectly. It definitely did mean everything to him just to be her man.

They eventually made it back to the room, and Lucy collapsed in the chair. "What a day…and night," she told Cal. "I've known you for nine months, and you never mentioned you can play a guitar?"

He smiled at her. "I like to have you discover my talents, one at a time."

He knelt in front of her again and unbuckled her shoes. She put her hands on his face and kissed him.

Later, when he held her in his arms, he asked, "Lucy, do you miss this life with all of the excitement and the challenges? I am constantly afraid I will lose you to this someday."

She raised up on one elbow so she could look into his eyes. "Listen to me, Calvin Frasier. I realize your mother left your father to go back to New York, but I will never do that. You will not lose me unless you ask me to leave. I love you more than I can ever tell you, and I would never want to go back to my old life. Why do you worry that I will?"

"You seem to be able to slip in and out of this world with little effort. It frightens me that one day you will step back into it and not come back to me."

She ran her fingers through his hair. "That will never happen. I promise I will be with you until one of us leaves this world behind."

With a soft groan of satisfaction, Lucy rolled off Cal's body and lay next to him. With his arm cradling her, she placed her head on his chest so she could listen to his strong heartbeat.

"Will it always be like this, Cal? Will we always be this infatuated with each other?"

"Yes, I think we will. Why do you ask?"

"Every time you touch me, every fiber of my being wants to make love to you. I want that desire to continue until we are 80 or 90…forever."

"Well, Abraham and Sarah were still making love when they were 100, so I think we have a good shot at it," Cal teased. "I don't think that feeling will ever fade, Lucy."

"Mmmm, I certainly hope not. I love loving you and being loved by you, Cowboy."

* * *

A few mornings later, Lucy pulled on a pair of shorts and a tank top. When she walked through the kitchen, Cal and Ben were sitting at the table with their laptops and a stack of papers.

"You guys look industrious this morning. What's all this?" she asked motioning to the papers as she pulled a bottle of water from the refrigerator.

Ben was using a calculator and frowning. "We're working on ratios for rate of gain in the spring calves. And trying to figure out when this whole rustling scheme might happen or what they're waiting for."

"Why aren't you doing this in that beautiful office you have at the end of the stables?" Lucy asked.

Ben looked at Cal. "Yeah, Dad, why aren't we doing this paperwork in the office?"

"All right, all right, I can take a hint. I'll make it my first priority to clean the office and get it back in some semblance of order," Cal told both of them.

Cal turned to look at Lucy. "I'm going to ask the same thing . . . what's all this?" He indicated the running clothes and the headband she put on.

"I didn't like what I saw in the mirror this morning," Lucy said as she patted her midsection, "so I'm going to do a little running or walking in the mornings, before it's unbearably hot."

Ben looked up from his laptop. "The doctor told Candy she should walk every day, but so far, she hasn't. I think she needs some motivation. Maybe she could walk with you, Lucy."

"I think when I was pregnant, I lacked motivation, too. Being pregnant in the summer is not lots of fun, especially when it's this hot outside. You really should plan better for the next 11 children, Ben." She laughed, kissed Cal on the cheek, and went out the door.

She walked across the great room and knocked softly on Candy's door. Lucy heard her say, "Come in."

"Candy, Ben said your doctor suggested you do some walking. Would you like to join me? I promise no power walking. We will take it slow and easy while it's still cool."

Candy looked like the last thing she wanted to do was walk somewhere, but she agreed and slipped her feet into her shoes.

"Here, Honey, let me tie your shoes for you," Lucy offered when she realized it was going to be a struggle for Candy to bend over and tie them.

"I really shouldn't be this big yet. The doctor says it is a large, healthy baby. No twins, but I feel like I'm carrying triplets. He wants me to walk because my legs are swelling, and he says it will help with the delivery, too."

"I'm sure he's right, but he's not the one carrying that basketball around, is he?" Lucy laughed.

"I don't remember you walking every day, Lucy. Is this something new?" Candy asked as they headed down the drive.

"Yes," Lucy sighed while she grabbed the same small roll of flesh at her midsection. "I looked in the mirror and didn't like what I saw. I guess instead of walking, I should follow Cal around all day and do whatever he does to keep that washboard stomach he has."

"Yeah, Ben commented about what good shape his dad is in. Of course, he says it's all because of you, Lucy. You keep him young."

Lucy smiled. "I don't know if I can take credit for that, but speaking of Cal's age, he has a birthday coming up. I thought maybe we could celebrate the Fourth of July and his birthday with a family cookout or something. I should probably call everybody now before they make other plans." They continued down the drive. "Ben mentioned your parents would like to come when the baby is born?"

Candy sighed deeply. "I don't even want to think about it. It would be a disaster on so many levels. My parents definitely do not get along even though they've been divorced for many years. If you had to spend time around them, you would think they got a divorce last week. Time has certainly not healed all wounds."

"Neither one ever remarried?" Lucy asked.

"No. Truthfully, I always prayed they might resolve their differences and get back together, but it's time to be realistic about the whole thing. I don't want them here. Maybe it would work out after the baby is a few months old and if they come one at a time. Daddy is very protective of me, since I was the baby and the only girl after four boys. I know he would try telling everyone how to take care of me and thinking he knew more than the doctors or anyone else, even Ben. Mom is bossy, too, but in a different way. We never had a close relationship. She had five children, but by the time she got to me, she didn't want to change diapers or fix bottles any more. I think Daddy did most of that…for me, at least."

"So, can you suggest they wait and come later?"

"I don't know if I can or not. Ben says we should let them come, and he'll make sure they don't upset me. I trust him to do that, but I don't think it's fair to ask him to do it."

They walked for another half hour. Lucy asked, "Are you ready to go back, Candy? I don't want to wear you out on our first walk. We can go again tomorrow if you want to. It's getting pretty warm."

They turned and retraced their steps back to the house. After Lucy made sure Candy was settled and had something to drink, she went back to her house.

Chapter 13

BEN AND CAL WERE STILL AT THE TABLE, looking pretty satisfied with themselves.

"So, what have you two discovered?" Lucy asked as she stood behind Cal and massaged his shoulders.

"Ben and I think we've figured out how the rustling is going to happen and how they can possibly hope to accomplish it in one night. What we don't know is probably the most important piece of the puzzle—when this will happen."

"Really? So tell me what you know. I'm interested," Lucy said.

Ben told her, "It is virtually impossible to load all the stock in one night, so they are going to have to decide what is going to hurt us the most, financially. We ran lots of figures and decided they will probably take the feeder calves, for several reasons. First, they can pack more of them into a trailer, because they're obviously smaller than the breeding stock."

"A bull rack can legally carry 50,000 pounds. They'll probably add a few thousand pounds and take the back roads around the scales. They'll have to double-deck them, which they couldn't do with adult cattle. The calves will be easier to load, also. I'm sure they'll bring portable loading chutes they can set up quickly," Cal continued.

"The price of feeder calves has been rising steadily over the past few weeks. I'm fairly certain they're waiting for it to go even higher. Not to mention, we sell to the same buyers every year. Our buyers know our stock to be healthy and have a good weight gain potential. If we have nothing to sell them this year, we'll lose them as customers. That will hurt us, too."

Lucy questioned them, "So stealing the calves would hurt you more than the breeding stock? I would think it would be the other way around."

Cal explained, "They won't separate the bull calves from the heifers, so they will be depleting next year's young breeding stock, too. It would affect the herd for several years. That could ruin some ranchers financially."

"Did you look at the papers I got from Roberto?" Lucy asked. "Did the name of the guy calling the shots for Carmion ring a bell?"

Cal stood and ran his fingers through his hair. "Yes, unfortunately, it did. He's one of the top men in the cattle association, and he undoubtedly had a hand in the removal of the ranger from this county. And the financing is coming from one of the biggest cattle buyers in the southwest. There sure are a lot of people with their fingers in this pie. They must all stand to make a huge profit off the subdividing of our two ranches, which are considered *small* for Texas ranches."

"Think about it, Dad," Ben said. "This is prime property for people who want to live on mini-farms, have a few horses, and still be able to commute to Houston or any of the surrounding towns for their work. It's a perfect location, and while we don't own hundreds of thousands of acres, we own the right amount for their purposes. They stand to profit millions of dollars."

Lucy asked one more question. "What about our friend, Patricia, Cal? She's involved in this, too."

Cal replied, "She keeps calling me. I ignore it and don't answer."

"I think you need to meet with her. Answer the next time she calls and set up a meeting. See what she wants."

Cal looked at her in astonishment. "You really want me to meet with her?"

Lucy looked him in the eyes. "There's an old saying that says, 'Sometimes you have to meet the devil face-to-face.'"

As she left the kitchen, she added, "But there's no old saying that says you have to sleep with the devil."

* * *

After the guys left, Lucy decided to call Jerry and see if there was anything new concerning the biological father of Bethany and Devon. His secretary answered and said he wouldn't be in the office until next week.

"That seems strange," she commented. "I thought he was going to work on the adoption case."

"I'm not supposed to tell everyone, but I'm sure he wouldn't mind if I told you, Mrs. Frasier."

"Told me what?" Lucy asked.

"He's in Las Vegas, and I'm pretty sure he got married to someone."

Lucy nearly dropped the phone. Then she started laughing and couldn't stop. "Thank you for sharing that with me," she managed to say between gasps for breath. "I'll call him next week." It took a while for the information to sink in.

Once she recovered and could speak coherently again, she called her daughter-in-law. "Hi, Samantha. I'm calling to check on you. Are you doing okay?"

"Yes, I'm surviving. Sean hasn't moved back home yet, but that's probably better for both of us. He did agree to go to counseling, so we're taking it one day at a time."

"That's a good thing, Samantha. Don't rush it. I'm happy to hear about counseling. Your dad will be happy to hear that, too. Can I share with him?"

"Of course, Lucy. Tell him to keep praying about the whole situation, too, okay?"

"I will. Speaking of your father, I'd like to have a birthday party for him. Since his birthday is on the second, we can celebrate the Fourth of July and his birthday on the same day. Please tell Sean he is welcome, also."

I'll tell him. I can't guarantee he'll come. He might feel uncomfortable."

"I do understand that. Whatever he decides is fine," Lucy assured her.

* * *

While she was on a roll with phone calls, Lucy dialed Jackie's number.

"Hi Jackie. I wondered if you chose a date for the baby shower yet. You might have to plan things that don't require Candy to move much because she is, in her words, 'as big as a barn.'"

Jackie didn't answer for a few seconds. Then she said quietly, "Lucy, I can't think of any way to say this gracefully so here it is. I'm pregnant. We found out a few weeks ago. It definitely wasn't planned, but after what we were told yesterday about Gabe, I truly wish I wasn't. I'm so distraught; I'm seriously contemplating ending this pregnancy. Gary doesn't want me to, but I think I have to."

For the second time within 30 minutes, Lucy was speechless. The difference was that one time was a result of joy and this time was due to being devastated for Jackie and Gary. "Jackie, listen to me, please. That isn't a decision you can make in a hurry. You and Gary have time to think and pray about this, okay? If I can ask, what did you find out about Gabe that was so upsetting to you?"

Jackie started to cry. "Our pediatrician suggested we have him tested for various things because he still isn't talking and he hasn't reached other milestones he should have at his age and he doesn't interact with other children, not even his cousins, who he knows. The results were explained to us yesterday. He has been diagnosed with autism. I don't know lots about it, but I know he'll never be normal, and I don't want to take the chance that another child would have it, too."

Lucy could hear the desperation in Jackie's voice. "Would you like me to come to your house for a while? I feel so helpless with this phone between us."

"Thank you, but it isn't necessary. Gary is coming home from work. I can't stop crying. I don't think I will ever stop crying."

Lucy realized she didn't know much about autism, either, but she did remember conversations with one of her plumbing contractors in Chicago who had a son with autism. Perhaps Anthony still had his contact information. She would ask when he and Emma came to dinner that evening.

One more call to Lynne. "Hi Lynne. How's everything with my Oklahoma family?"

"Hi Lucy. We are good. The kids are having a fun summer, but they truly miss being able to run to Grammy's house."

"I miss that, too, more than I can tell you. I wish you lived next door. Does Paul still like his job?"

"Yes, he does, especially the working from home part of it."

"So, is that a good thing? With homeschooling Annie and Jarrod, you never can escape all of them, can you?" Lucy laughed.

"It does get crazy some days," Lynne answered. "We're still looking for a larger house. We would like to find something before it's time to re-sign the lease."

"Maybe you should consider moving to Texas since Paul works from home," Lucy joked.

"Perhaps we should. I'm sorry that once again, I am the only one home. The kids will be sad they missed you."

"Tell them I will try to call tomorrow. We're having guests for dinner tonight so I should get busy working on that," Lucy told her. "One more thing…do you think you might be able to come for the Fourth of July? We are celebrating Cal's birthday that day, too, and I miss y'all so much."

Lynne told her she would talk to Paul about it and let her know.

Chapter 14

LUCY TIED THE STRINGS of her apron and started on the chili she was making for dinner. She would make macaroni and cheese for Vicki and the children. If Vicki ate the fiery chili, poor Olivia would be up all night with a bellyache, and it was probably too spicy for Bethany and Devon, too. Vicki would actually be thrilled with the mac and cheese. When she and Paul were children, they would have eaten it every day of the week if she had prepared it that often. That was a good thing, since many days that was all there was to eat. Then it was the quick and easy kind out of the box. Now she made the real thing with four kinds of cheese.

While she worked, her thoughts wandered back to the time when she was married to John and the kids were little. He worked such long hours some days; it was like being a single mother. Then when he got sick with the lung cancer brought on by all the paint fumes from his work, she felt guilty about having to spend so much time at the hospital and not with Paul and Vicki. After he died, she tried to make up for lost time, but unfortunately, some things can never be regained, and time is one of them.

They had both grown up to be responsible, industrious, well-adjusted adults, despite her failures. She silently thanked God for guiding them to the right life-mates and for bringing them back into his family.

She put the chili into the slow cooker to simmer for the rest of the day. It wasn't time to make the salad or the cornbread yet. She walked across the great room to visit Candy and see if there was anything she could do for her.

"Yes," Candy laughed. "You can have this baby for me."

"Well, that might not be possible, but perhaps I could make something for your dinner tonight."

"Lucy, Ben is so good to me. He works all day and then he comes in and does everything in here, too. I feel guilty and so thankful."

Lucy smiled at her daughter-in-law. "Ben is a wonderful husband, Candy. He loves you beyond words. It shows in his eyes every time he looks at you. He'll be a terrific father, too. I'm sure of it."

Candy started to cry. "I seem to cry at every little thing."

"It's okay, Sweetie. You're allowed to do that when you're pregnant. It's a privilege that comes with the territory. If you're certain Ben will have it all under control and you don't need me for anything, I'll go back to my house and get ready for company. Anthony and his wife, Emma, are in town to do some work at Vicki and David's house. They have a rental car, but I asked them to follow David out here. I was too lazy to try giving them directions," Lucy explained.

* * *

Cal came in a few hours later. He looked at her apron and commented, "Aren't you just the domesticated little housewife?"

"Listen, Calvin Frasier. Domesticated is the opposite of wild. Are you suggesting I used to be wild and now you have domesticated me?"

Cal scooped her into his arms and kissed her. "Lucy, you will always be wild. But it's okay; I like my women wild."

She pushed him away, laughing. "Go take a shower and wash the dust off, Cowboy. I'll show you wild…later."

"I can hardly wait," he said as he removed his boots and walked down the hall.

Lucy prepared the salad and slid the cornbread into the oven.

When Cal came back into the kitchen, she told him, "Cal, I have so many things to tell you but there isn't time before dinner. I will tell you this: Jerry and Phoebe got married in Vegas." She collapsed on a chair in another spasm of laughter. Cal looked at her for a minute to determine if she was teasing him, then smiled and nodded his head. "I'm happy for them."

It was good to see Anthony and Emma again. Cal offered a cold beer to all the adults but Vicki. He said it was a necessity to quench the fire if you were going to eat Lucy's chili. Vicki was thrilled with macaroni and cheese. "Wait until I tell Paul what you made for me for dinner tonight," Vicki said.

Lucy told Emma, "It's hard to believe anyone could get that excited about macaroni and cheese."

Cal asked God's blessings on the food and the people seated around the table.

After dinner, Cal took the children and Emma to the stables to see the horses, David and Vicki sat on the porch swing with Olivia, and Lucy and Anthony went for a walk around the house and barns. She explained the bunkhouse and the foreman's home and briefly touched on the rustling threat.

"So, Louisa, it was a good decision to marry your cowboy and move to Texas?"

"The best decision I've ever made, Anthony. I don't miss Chicago or the business at all."

"Are you certain of that, Louisa? I was talking to Cal before dinner. You know, he is worried about you and afraid this life may not be exciting enough for you some day."

"I don't know why he's worried. He asks me often if I'm happy here. I don't know how to ease his fears."

"Have you stepped back into that world you say you don't miss?"

Lucy frowned. "A few times, but it was always to help him keep this ranch that is his heritage."

Anthony stopped walking and turned to look at her. "Listen to me. I saw the way he looks at you. I can tell you he would rather lose every acre of land he has than lose you. Stay on this side of that invisible fence Louisa. He's afraid you will step over one day and not come back."

"Those are the exact words he used to describe his fears, Anthony. I don't know if I can watch something disastrous happen and do nothing if I know I could help."

"You will have to choose, Louisa. You can't forever live with one foot in each world. It will kill your marriage or possibly…you."

Everyone congregated on the porch. Ben and Candy joined them. Lucy stood with her arm around Cal's waist and nodded her head in the direction of Ben who was holding Olivia. "It won't be long before he's holding his own baby."

Anthony gave Lucy the contact information for the young man with the son with autism, and everyone went home except Bethany and Devon, who were going to stay until the security system was installed.

***

When they were tucked in for the night, Lucy curled up beside Cal on the couch with her head on his shoulder.

"So what are all the things you have to tell me, Lucy?" he asked.

She explained her call to Samantha and that she had specifically asked Cal to continue to pray for her and Sean's marriage. Then she told him about the heartbreaking conversation with Jackie.

"She can't be serious about aborting that baby, can she?" he asked.

"She's terribly upset about Gabe and the autism diagnosis. From her comment, I don't think she's had time to process it yet. She has no information, no organizations to contact, and no support groups. If she can get a grip on her feelings of helplessness, I think she will change her mind about the pregnancy. I know Jackie would never feel that way under normal circumstances, but right now it may be the only thing she feels she has any control over. Unfortunately, that isn't the kind of news you can work through quickly. I have the number of a man who worked for me in Chicago. He has a son with autism. I'll call and talk to him to learn a little more."

She felt Cal's body tense when she said that. "It's okay, Honey. He's one of the good guys from my past. No danger there, just helpful conversation."

She relayed the news of Paul's job and the fact that their house was too small. "Cal, what do you think about offering them the house on the Frasier Ranch? You said it should have someone living in it. They could certainly afford the rent, and it would be more than big enough for them. Since he works from home, it wouldn't matter where they lived."

Cal smiled, "And the last member of our family would be close to us, right?"

"Yes. Yes, they would. Can I suggest it to them if they come for your birthday party?"

"Of course. I think it's a great idea, and they can see it while they're here. You know, they do not have to pay any rent, Lucy."

"I know, but I don't think Paul will agree if it's free, you know? We will have to set some sort of rental price."

"We can work out the details after we know if they're interested or not. Now tell me about the apron. I have never seen you wear one. You shocked me when I walked in."

"You know I don't cook too often, but when I do, I end up ruining my clothes, so I thought I would dig out one of Grandma's aprons from a storage container upstairs and save my shirt from stains," Lucy explained. "Domesticated, indeed," she teased as she kissed his neck.

Cal suddenly stood up, grabbed Lucy around her waist, threw her over his shoulder and walked down the hall to their bedroom. "Come on, wild woman, I'm taking you with me."

* * *

"Lucy, are you coming with me to talk to that man your friend at the Illinois State Attorney's office told us to contact in Houston?" Cal asked the next morning.

"No, Sweetheart. You can handle it all by yourself. Besides, did you forget we have two children here for a few days?"

Cal chuckled, "I guess I did forget. I wish you could come along. I'm sure you're better at this than I am."

"Absolutely not—you're the rancher. Tell him what's going on and whom you suspect is involved, including Patricia. I know you'll handle it better than I ever could. You know cattle, remember? That includes 'cattle people' and how they think."

Cal nodded. "I think I'll swing through Beaumont on my way home and talk to Jackie if she's there and will talk to me."

Lucy kissed him good-bye and wished him luck.

Chapter 15

AFTER BREAKFAST, Bethany and Devon wanted to see the horses. "Yes, let's go now. It will be too hot this afternoon," Lucy told them. The heat had appeared with a vengeance. The central air never shut off, but it was possible to be out for an hour or so in the early morning.

Even though the chores had been done earlier by a ranch hand, Lucy allowed Devon and Bethany to add a little grain and hay and help refill the water buckets. They treated the horses to a few carrots. Watching them caused Lucy to smile; she could see herself doing those things when she was Devon's age. She promised a ride in the evening, as it was already becoming too hot.

Before she took them back to the house, she caught sight of a pick-up truck in her peripheral vision, disappearing around the end of the stable. She hurried the children to Ben and Candy's door. Without knocking, she opened it. Ben was still home helping Candy.

"Candy, please keep the kids in here for a little while. Lock the door. I'll explain later. Ben, can you come with me?"

"What is it?" Ben asked, as he instinctively reached for his holster and picked up his gun.

"I think I just saw the kids' father drive around the end of the stable."

"Did he go down the drive to the road?" Ben asked as he shaded his eyes and looked in that direction.

"I don't know for sure, but I don't think so. He may be parked on the far side, waiting for us to go inside."

Ben thought for a minute. "I'll go around this way, and you go around that side like you're out for a morning walk. We'll see if he's still here."

Lucy looked at Ben and raised her palms. "And then what?" she asked. "What if he's armed?"

Ben took the safety off his gun and shrugged his shoulders. "I guess we'll find out."

Lucy tried to look nonchalant as she rounded the end of the stable. The front bumper of a rusty red truck was visible, parked on the far end. As she walked closer, Ben approached from the far side, yanked the door open and pulled a young man out of the cab.

"Who are you and what are you doing here?" Ben asked while holding him by his shirt.

"Don't shoot me, please. My name's Blake Tanner. I just wanted to see my kids."

Lucy looked at him closely. "Blake Tanner? I thought you said your name was Carlos the last time we met, Mr. Tanner."

"I know. I lied to you. I didn't want you to know who I really was." He was still being held by Ben. He had no weapon on him. Ben let go of his shirt but didn't put the gun away.

"You're trespassing, you know. You have no business here, kids or not."

Ben told Lucy, "I'll call the sheriff's department. They can come get him."

Ben handed Lucy his pistol. "I'll search his truck. If he tries to run, shoot him in the leg."

Then he looked at the young man in front of him. "Don't be stupid and think she can't or won't shoot you. I guarantee she will."

* * *

A deputy arrived and asked a few questions. He told Ben he would call a towing company to take the truck to impound. Then he cuffed Blake Tanner, put him in the car, and drove off.

Sweat was running off Lucy's face by now. Not only was it unbearably hot, but she was thinking how close the kids had come to possibly being taken. The thought made her sick to her stomach. She would tell Vicki and David, but not this morning.

Lucy settled the children in front of the TV to watch a movie while she changed clothes.

"How would you two like to help me bake cookies?" she asked. "We can take some to Aunt Candy and Uncle Ben when they're done, okay?"

"Can't we eat some too?" Bethany pouted.

"Yes, of course, Bethany. The cook always gets the first cookies. It's a rule."

Devon helped gather the ingredients, and Bethany pulled a chair to the counter.

Amid much giggling and spilling of ingredients, the cookie dough was mixed. Lucy thought of the many times she had made cookies with Jarrod and Annie. She missed them. The finished cookies were delicious. They each ate several and enjoyed glasses of cold milk to wash them down.

"Let's take some to Uncle Ben's house, like you said, Gramma," Devon suggested.

"Okay. I'll put some on a plate. Do you think you can carry them without letting them slide off?" Lucy asked.

"I want my own plate to carry," Bethany insisted. Lucy fixed another plate for her to carry. Bethany definitely had a mind of her own, and many times it got her into lots of trouble.

After lunch, both kids took a nap which allowed Lucy to do some planning for Cal's birthday party.

Paul called to say they would be able to attend the party on the Fourth of July. Lucy told him about the proposal of them moving to the other ranch house and asked him to think about it and discuss it with Lynne. He was totally surprised but didn't immediately discount the idea, which Lucy thought was a good sign.

Victoria called and told her Anthony was finishing up with the installation of the security system and would probably be leaving for home on Sunday. Lucy asked if they could keep Bethany and Derek until church on Sunday. Vicki agreed and invited them to come for dinner after church.

"Vicki, do the children know they are adopted? I'm not saying they *should* know; I just want to be sure I don't say or do the wrong thing concerning that situation."

"David and I have discussed it briefly with them. We probably would have waited until they were older, especially Bethany, but it was obviously a topic of conversation at the foster home where they were for quite some time. Have they brought it up?"

"No, but I want to be prepared if either of them do." She made the decision to tell David and Vicki about Blake Tanner on Sunday. Besides, she wanted to get Cal's perspective first.

Sometimes it amazed her how much she relied on Cal's opinion and wisdom. If anyone had asked her before she met him if she could envision anything like that, the answer would have been an emphatic, "No." She had prided herself on being self-reliant and making all her own decisions. *Loving someone intensely definitely changes things,* she mused.

* * *

Cal called to say he would be late and not to wait for him for dinner. He stopped to see Samantha and Jackie, and he had lots of news about the whole "rustling thing" as he called it. Lucy could hardly wait to hear everything he found out.

After the children ate, she kept her promise to let them ride for a little bit. It had cooled down some, and Candy and Ben were on their front porch. Ben asked quietly if she wanted him to stay with her in case their father was out on bail.

Lucy told him he didn't have to come along, but she was going to let them ride in the front drive, so if he wanted to stay on the porch it would make her feel safer. Devon wanted to keep the reins in his hands while Lucy walked beside him, but Bethany needed Lucy to hang on to her as they walked, even though she wanted to do it by herself.

Before they were done riding, Cal drove in. He kissed Lucy, then picked up Devon and Bethany while Lucy took care of Nell and returned her to her stall. They all walked to the porch where Ben and Candy were still sitting.

"After the kids are in bed, you might want to come over, and I'll tell you what I found out today. Most of it is good news, I think. I was having a hard time wrapping my mind around some of it."

* * *

Cal ate some dinner while Lucy prepared their baths. "I don't want to take a bath," Bethany said as she stomped her foot for emphasis.

"Oh, Honey, you have to. You smell like a horse, and you don't want to go to bed like that."

"Yes, I do. I like that smell, Gramma Lucy. I want to smell like my horse."

Lucy smiled as she remembered almost those exact words coming out of her mouth when her grandma wanted her to take a bath. Some things never change. She finally persuaded Bethany to get in the tub. When they were both ready for bed, Cal tucked them in and said prayers with them.

They sat together so he could tell her about his visits with his daughters before discussing the news he wanted to share with Ben and Candy.

"When I stopped at Samantha's house, Sean was there. I didn't act surprised, although I was…sort of. We visited for a while about everyday things. Then Sean apologized to me for hurting Samantha and asked for my forgiveness. Truthfully, he caught me off guard. I didn't expect that at all. I told him I forgave him, but I wasn't the one who needed to forgive him. He said he had asked for God's forgiveness and of course, for Samantha's, but he wanted mine, also. I told him I respected him for being so honest."

"Has he moved back home?" Lucy asked.

"I don't believe so, but they are continuing to go to counseling. I think it's a good thing to take it slow and not rush back. They will appreciate each other more in the long run."

Cal sighed before continuing. "Then I went to Jackie's. She is still pretty upset. You know, I wanted to put her on my lap and talk it over with her like I did when she was a little girl, but she isn't a little girl any longer. She's a grown woman who needs some guidance on this journey right now. We discussed Gabe. I told her you were going to talk to someone who has a son with autism and perhaps could give her some perspective on the situation. She knows how I feel about abortion, and she feels that way, too, but right now, her emotions are spinning out of control. She and Gary did pray with me, asking for God's guidance and making good decisions. She knows we love her and will help in any way we can so I will leave it up to God. He's much wiser than me."

While they waited for Ben and Candy to join them, Lucy asked, "I've been waiting for the chance to ask you about your guitar playing. You surprised me at the hotel. When did you learn to play?"

Cal smiled at the memory. "When I was in high school, a few friends and I decided we wanted to have a band. They actually played, but I had never even held a guitar before that. My mom agreed to a few lessons to see if I would stick with it, and after learning some basic chords, I was pretty much self-taught. We had fun for a while, but then we all went our separate ways, and our band disintegrated. In college, I met a guy who seriously needed a guitar player for his group. This was a band that actually got paid to play at weddings and in some small bars. I practiced and played with them all through college. I still have my guitar, packed away upstairs somewhere. After Kathy died, I never played again until I played for you in the hotel. It felt good to pick it up again. Now that we have a whole passel of grandkids, it might be fun to play for them sometimes like I used to play for my kids."

"You know," he continued, "the best thing the group did for me didn't have anything to do with playing in clubs. They all belonged to a church group that was going on a mission trip and invited me to go along. I truthfully didn't care about the *missions* part of it, but a trip to Guatemala sounded like a great experience. It *was* a great experience because I met Christ and accepted him as my Savior on that trip, and we've had a relationship ever since."

Ben came in and sat with them. He said Candy was too tired and had gone to bed.

"Okay, are you ready for all this?" Cal asked, smiling like the cat that swallowed the canary.

"It seems the legal 'powers that be' are already quite aware of Carmion's illegal activities but haven't been able to prove anything yet. They didn't know about the involved person on the board of the cattle association but were anxious to start that investigation...thank you, Lucy, for that information. They also know the ranger for this county was removed and not replaced. They are going to leave it that way for now to avoid arousing suspicion. Sheriff Ganger is indeed covering the rustler's tracks. He obviously didn't think his pension was going to keep him happy in his retirement and wanted more. Greed is a powerful thing and leads to many bad decisions. In his case, illegal decisions. The 'deputy' who was here with him is the grandson of the original Double K owner, as you suspected, Lucy. Patricia is his sister. She came here to be closer to our operation and collect any information she could. They forced the man who leased the Frasier ranch to move out so she could move in. When I didn't lease the ranch house to her, she started making calls to me to meet her somewhere. As I told you, Lucy, I never answered, but now they want me to meet with her and see what she wants."

"And wear a wire, correct?" Lucy asked.

"Yes. I can't even begin to tell you how uncomfortable I am with that. Not only the whole 'wire' thing but just meeting her for dinner. I don't want to go to dinner with anyone but you."

"Anyway, they want us to keep the calves in an accessible pasture so the rustlers will actually load them and drive off the ranch with them."

"Isn't that sort of dangerous? What if they keep going and take them across state lines? We'll lose all of them," Ben reasoned.

"That's a chance we'll have to take if we want to stop this. If they don't physically leave the ranch with the calves, some expensive lawyer will call it trespassing and nothing more.

There's a rancher on the Oklahoma border that lost 75 percent of his herd before anyone was aware of this operation. They are concentrating on land that could be used for development, of course, but seem to have a special vendetta against our ranches. I'm sure it is as you said, Lucy. The grandson, whose real name is Caleb, by the way, has a burning hatred for me due to the fact he thinks he could have been a millionaire a long time ago if I hadn't bought the Yellow Rose from Leon instead of letting his grandfather buy it."

"So what do we do now besides keep the calves in the right pasture?" Ben asked.

"We wait. There will be special cattle rangers who will be staying in a hotel in Magnolia during the day. They will come out here at night and sort of 'camp out' where they can survey the pasture where they think this is going to go down. They are certain it will be within the next week. Once the trucks roll out, they will radio the State Police, and they can stop them. Hopefully, all goes according to plan. The only part of the plan I don't like is meeting with Patricia."

"You'll do great, Sweetheart. Remember I told you sometimes you have to meet the devil face-to-face. I think you're going to meet him in female form."

CHAPTER 16

LUCY REALIZED THE NEXT MORNING at breakfast that she had not told Cal about the visit from Blake Tanner and their exciting morning.

"So where is he now?" he asked after hearing what had happened.

"I don't know. I hope he's still in jail, but I suppose he could have posted bail. It couldn't be too much for just trespassing, right?"

Cal shook his head. "It's no wonder people become overwhelmed with life. I feel like I'm aging about a year every day. Maybe I'll really be 73 on my birthday instead of 63. Wouldn't it be nice to have a time when everything is right in our world, Lucy? I don't want to play spy games or worry about my cattle and land being stolen from me or Bethany and Devon taken by their father or Jackie and Gabe or Samantha and Sean's problems. I want to get up some morning, drink coffee with you, ride Cutter to check on the cattle and horses, and come back home and make love to you all day. That sounds like the perfect day to me."

"I like that picture, too, but I'm afraid until we reach heaven, there will always be troubles in our lives. It does seem the troubles are in double digits right now. When the rustling scenario is over, the other things might resolve themselves. In the meantime, we'll have to catch glimpses of happiness. Although, being with you makes me happy every day, Cowboy."

Cal smiled at Lucy's use of her pet name for him. She made everything else in life bearable. He kissed her soundly before he heard the kids getting up and coming down the hall to the kitchen.

Devon said, "Bethany wet her bed, Gramma Lucy. She does that sometimes."

Bethany was rubbing her eyes and slowly coming to Lucy. "It's okay, Sweetheart. Come here." Lucy threw a blanket over her legs before she lifted Bethany onto her lap. Her pajamas were, indeed, quite damp. She snuggled this little girl who had been in several homes in her short life. It made her heart hurt.

"Are you my real Gramma?" Bethany asked.

"Yes, I am your real Gramma, Bethany. Why are you asking?"

Devon chose to answer that question around a mouthful of cereal Cal had fixed for him. "When we were in that other house, the lady there told us we should call her Mommy, and that her mom would come over and we had to call her Grandma. But she said our real mom was in jail, and she didn't know our real grandma. Then we went to our house where we live now. I told Bethany that's our real mom and dad now, but I don't think she believes me."

Lucy couldn't stop a few tears from running down her face as she looked at Cal over Bethany's head. This conversation was breaking her heart for these two little people who had been tossed about like rag dolls. If they had to meet Blake Tanner, too, what would that do to them? She was thanking God she had asked Vicki how much they knew about their adoption when she talked to her yesterday. It was no surprise Bethany had accidents at night. She probably had nightmares, too.

Lord, please give me the right words for Bethany and Devon, Lucy silently prayed before she spoke. "Bethany, do you remember when your mommy and daddy took you to the store to pick out a special doll, when you first came to their house?"

Bethany nodded her head. "I have her in my room. Her name is Mindy."

"You could have chosen any doll you wanted, but you chose Mindy. You wanted to take her home and cuddle her and be her 'mommy,' right?"

Again, Bethany nodded but didn't say anything.

"Well, your mommy and daddy chose you and Devon, too. They knew they wanted you to be with them forever."

"Did they get us at a store?" Bethany asked, her eyes wide at the thought.

Lucy chuckled. "No, not at a store but they still got to choose you. You are their real little girl, and Devon is their real little boy forever, just like Olivia is their real little girl. You are a very special family. I will be your Gramma Lucy and Grandpa will be your Grandpa Cal for the rest of your life."

Bethany seemed satisfied with that answer, at least for the moment. "Can I have some cereal now?"

"As soon as I hose you down in the shower and put dry clothes on you," Lucy told her.

While they were gone, Cal's phone rang. He took a deep breath and answered it.

When Lucy and Bethany returned to the kitchen, Cal put his arms around Lucy. "I have a date…with Patricia."

Lucy shivered. "When and where?"

"At The Acropolis Hotel in Houston, next Wednesday evening at 6. I will tell the ranger in charge of the investigation so they can get me dressed and wired and be on hand to rescue me."

"The Acropolis? Well, she certainly has expensive tastes. And in Houston? She wants you as far away from your comfort zone as possible. Sad to say, I totally understand this broad and where she's going, although when I used to negotiate, I wasn't doing anything illegal. This will be okay, Cal. You can do it. But please remember this: I'm not the only woman who carries a revolver in her purse or elsewhere."

"Did you ever have to wear a wire, as they call it?"

"Yes, during the two years of the drug trial, I wore one several times. You have to forget it's there or you'll give it away and not accomplish what you want to do."

"I don't want to play spy games, Lucy. I certainly don't want to play them with some other woman. I'm a rancher. How did this happen?"

Lucy laughed at him and assured him the drama would all be over soon, and he could go back to being her rancher husband.

* * *

In church on Sunday morning, the Old Testament reading was Psalm 27, verses 1-3.

The verses spoke of being confident in knowing God is the strength of our lives and there is no need to fear the wicked or our enemies. Even though war may break out and our foes surround us, God is with us and there is no need to fear.

Lucy entwined her fingers in Cal's and squeezed his hand. They both felt as though the Lord was speaking directly to their situation with these verses.

After church, they enjoyed dinner at David and Vicki's house with Anthony and Emma who were getting ready to fly back to Florida. Lucy walked them to their rental car. "I can't begin to thank you enough, Anthony. Once again, you have come to my rescue, in more ways than one. I thought long and hard about the things you told me that night at the ranch. You are right, of course. I am going to take your advice and stay on this side of that invisible fence with Cal, who means more to me than anything in this world." She hugged him and Emma and said good-bye.

When she came back inside, the children were watching a movie. Lucy told David and Vicki about the incident with Blake Tanner at the ranch.

All the color drained from Victoria's face. "I don't want to think about this happening. The fact that he's right here is scary to me. How will I ever go to the grocery or anything? He could be anywhere waiting to snatch them."

"Jerry should be back in his office tomorrow. Call him. He can find out if Mr. Tanner is still in jail or out on bond. I'm sure he will have news of some kind. The court should have ordered a paternity test by now. This will be resolved, Honey. I don't think their father has the resources to raise two young children. Continue to pray about it, and we will, too."

Cal told them about the proposal to Paul and Lynne to live in the house on the Frasier Ranch. That cheered Vicki up a bit. "I would love it if they would be closer. Oh, I hope they accept."

Chapter 17

AFTER SOME SEARCHING, Lucy found Cal's guitar in its case, packed away in the storage room. She planned to take it to town and drop it off to be restrung, repaired, tuned, and whatever else it needed as a surprise for his birthday. First, she had to sneak it out of the house.

After she left the music shop, she decided to see if Jerry was in his office and might have a few minutes to see her.

His receptionist told her he would be available in a bit. When he opened his office door, all she could do was smile at him. Then she hugged him, "I hear congratulations are in order, Jerry. How dare you kidnap my best friend and not let me know about it," she teased.

He shook his head as if he was still trying to believe it. "It was a sudden decision but unquestionably the best decision of my life, Lucy. And…we have you to thank for it."

"No, not really," she answered. "I just couldn't stand seeing two people I love be miserable, so my controlling self pushed you together. I can't wait to talk to Phoebe, but I have another question for you today."

"Okay, let's hear it."

"Is Blake Tanner still in jail, and if he is, would I be allowed to see him?"

"I called this morning to check on Mr. Tanner. He is still in jail because he can't post bond, even though it is very small. The paternity tests have been administered, and it seems he is the biological father of Devon and Bethany. Why do you want to see him, Lucy? Please tell me you aren't going to try to bribe him to leave. He will just return again and again for more money."

"I am not going to throw money at him. I'm smarter than that, Jerry; give me some credit, okay? I want to talk to him, that's all."

"There is no law against talking to him, but I am advising you not to do it. I don't think Victoria and David would be happy about it, either."

"I understand that, and your advice is duly noted, Jerry."

He looked at her over the top of his reading glasses and said, "And you are going anyway, aren't you?"

Lucy didn't answer him directly. "Please tell Phoebe I will call her this afternoon. We need to catch up on her new life."

Jerry watched her walk out, knowing she was on her way to see Blake Tanner. *Stubborn, obstinate woman,* he thought.

* * *

When Lucy sat across from a sullen Blake Tanner, she wasn't sure this had been a good idea after all. He glared at her and asked, "What do you want? Last time I saw you, you were threatening to shoot me, as I recall."

"That's true and as I recall, you were trespassing on private property looking to kidnap two children."

"I wasn't going to kidnap them. I just wanted to see them and talk to them a little. I didn't even know they existed until a few months ago. Wouldn't you want to see them if they were your children?" he asked her.

"Yes, I would, but I don't believe I would be so sneaky. I would work through the system. How does it happen you didn't know you had children?"

Blake took a deep breath. "After their mother and I paired up for a while, she disappeared. I figured she found somebody else so I moved on with my life; it wasn't like we were in love or anything. I lived in California for a while and one day, I was back in New Mexico and then I moved on to Texas. A former friend and I went out for the evening, and guess who was at the bar? We talked and drank for a while and left together. She was gone before I woke up the next morning, and I never saw her again. Yeah, you guessed it; she got pregnant again. Don't lecture me about birth control. I can tell you when you're as high as we were, it wasn't even on our radar."

"So, how did you find out about your children?"

"A friend of hers knew about the kids, and when their mother was sentenced to prison, her friend tried to contact me. I never had a permanent address, so it took a long time to catch up to me…months, years…I don't know. When I called her, she said their mother had given them up, and they had been adopted. She wasn't absolutely sure they were mine but said the oldest one looked like me, and their mother was sure they were mine but didn't want me to know."

Lucy studied this young man and almost felt sorry for him. What irreparable consequences can come from irresponsible choices, she thought.

She asked, "Blake, tell me, do you really believe you can provide for your children? At this point in your life, I mean. Raising children is expensive. Clothes, food, housing, medical attention—it all costs money. They have some emotional problems from being in the system and shuffled around. Do you think you can handle that or get them the help they need? Plus, correct me if I'm wrong, but you have a felony on your record, right?"

Blake's eyes narrowed, "So did you come here to make a list of my past sins or rub it in that I have no money and no job, unlike you, who have everything and whose life is perfect?"

Lucy smiled at him, "No, I didn't. And believe me, my life has not always been perfect, and I have not always had money. I'm here because I would like you to think about the consequences of your actions, previously and now. What happens if you take them and then you are constantly running from the law? You will spend your life looking over your shoulder because someone will be looking for you; you know that. If you care about them, even a little bit, and I believe you when you say you do, surely you can see the life they would be forced to live. Is that really what you want for them?"

"So what is your answer? Paying me to leave town?"

I can hardly wait to tell Jerry that he and Blake think along the same lines, she thought.

"No," Lucy said emphatically. "I am not here to offer you money. I'm trying to see if there might be another solution to this problem. My daughter and son-in-law do not deserve to live in fear of having you steal their children every day of their lives."

"*My* children," he corrected her.

Lucy was losing patience with him. "Yes, you're right. *Your* children, biologically. How much time did that take? About 15 minutes for each one, if you were lucky. Their mother was thinking about the best interests of her babies, and even though it was unimaginably difficult to sign her rights away, she did it. You need to take a lesson from her and think about the same thing. There are plans available that allow you to meet the adoptive parents and assess them. If you think they would be the best choice for your children, you can voluntarily relinquish your parental rights. There would be mediation available where you might even be able to receive a picture of them occasionally. I want you to think about that,

Blake, because I assure you I will use all that money you think I have, to fight you every step of the way if you want to pursue your efforts to take them. Do you understand me?"

Blake nodded.

"Good. I won't come back, but an attorney named Jerry Watkins will, and he can tell you about the mediation if you want to talk about it. One more thing, Blake, my suggestion is to ask for God's help to get some counseling for yourself, get clean, find a job and then…find a nice woman you can love and actually start a family you can provide for."

Lucy left the jail and knew she was going to be in all kinds of trouble with Jerry, Cal, Vicki, and David, but she wasn't sorry she went.

She stopped at Jerry's office to tell him what she had discussed with Blake. To say he was upset with her was probably an understatement.

"What did you hope to accomplish? Do you really think Vicki and David are going to meet him and do any mediating with him?"

"If they want to have any hope of disentangling themselves from this situation and moving on with their lives without being afraid every day, they darn well better meet with him," Lucy shouted.

Jerry looked at her. She really was a force of nature. Cal Frasier definitely married a strong woman, and he seemed to love every minute of it. Jerry shook his head, and then told her, "Okay, I will pursue the relinquishing rights mediation, but you, my dear, get to tell Vicki and David what you set up."

Lucy left his office and went straight to Vicki's. If she was going to have an entire day of being yelled at, she might as well get it over with.

She replayed the conversation with Blake Tanner for Vicki and David. Vicki looked as though she was going to throw her coffee cup at her. "What right do you have to meddle in this, Mom? Let Jerry handle it; that's what he gets paid for. I cannot believe you went to talk to Blake without talking to us first."

"I know, I know," Lucy said. "You know, sometimes it's better to commit the sin and ask for forgiveness than to ask for permission."

"Really?" David said. "Who told you that?"

"I don't know. Somebody in my past, I believe. Look, I apologize, but what did it hurt? If he says no to my suggestions, there's no harm done. You will still have to mess with this for a long time. If he thinks about it and agrees, it could all be over in a few weeks. He isn't going to see the children, just you two. If someone else was going to raise your children, wouldn't you at least like to talk to them and be at peace with the fact that they would be good parents?"

David looked at Vicki, who was still frowning at Lucy. "She has a good point, Honey. Maybe he will decide to give up his rights voluntarily. Then our lives could get back to some sort of normal, and we would never have to worry about anyone trying to take Bethany and Devon again."

"I suppose you're right, David. But, Mom, I'm still angry at you so don't think all is forgiven so quickly."

Lucy took that as her cue to leave and go home where she could explain it all again to Cal, who would probably lecture her, too. She smiled and thought, *I don't care. It was the best idea, and one day, they will all figure that out. I hope.*

* * *

Jerry locked the door to his office and hurried home. This was the first period in his life he was eager to go home. Before it was always a lonely feeling to come home to an empty house, but now that Phoebe would be waiting for him, it was a joy to walk in the door.

"Hey, Baby, how was your day?" he asked as he walked through the door.

Phoebe met him in the hallway and kissed him. "It was lonesome and boring, but it's good now that you're here."

"I know and I'm sorry, Phoebe. We will pick out a new car for you tomorrow, I promise. I'm sorry everything was left in Illinois. You can sell your car there, and you can decide what you want to do about your printing business and your house, okay?"

Phoebe smiled at him. "It's okay, Jerry. I was teasing you about being bored. I spent part of the day cooking a gourmet meal for you. I tried calling Lucy, but she wasn't answering."

Jerry chuckled, "No, she couldn't answer because she was talking to a young man at the jail, and phones aren't allowed in there."

"At the jail? Who does she know at the jail?" Phoebe asked.

"Actually, she doesn't know anyone but felt the need to have a discussion with an inmate. Against my advice, I might add."

"Really? Well, that doesn't surprise me, I guess. Lucy doesn't always take advice if she's on a mission."

"No kidding," Jerry laughed. "I'm pretty sure she caught all kinds of flak from Vicki and David, but if I'm honest, she did everyone a favor, I think. She probably set the plans in motion for a quick resolution to the adoption issue. But don't tell her I said that, okay? I think she missed her calling. She should have been a police negotiator or something similar, maybe an attorney. She has an uncanny ability to cut through all kinds of superfluous 'stuff' and get to the heart of an issue."

"Sort of like the night at my house, right? I was going to tell you I couldn't see you again until she forced me…and I mean that literally…to talk to you."

Jerry moved to her and wrapped his arms around her. "And just how do we ever thank her for that, Phoebe? I can't imagine missing out on your love for the rest of my life."

"I don't know, but I will always be indebted to her."

Chapter 18

SUDDENLY IT WAS WEDNESDAY. The calves had been moved to the pasture that Cal and Ben believed was the most easily accessible by semi-trucks and trailers. The rangers would be ready as they had been for several nights, although they believed it was going to happen when Patricia had Cal occupied in Houston.

When he was ready to leave, Lucy and Ben walked out with him. "How long will it take them to get me ready for this meeting?" he asked Lucy.

"Not too long, maybe 30 minutes to hook you up and give you some instructions. It's easier to hide a wire on a man than a woman." When he looked questioningly at her, she explained, "A man usually has more clothes on than a *woman on the prowl* does."

He kissed her longingly and then whispered, "Please pray for me and this whole crazy situation, Lucy. I just want to come home to you."

"I will, I promise. You will come home to me, Cal. Now go, before we both decide you should stay here."

As he drove down the drive, Ben said, "You know, I feel sorry for Dad. He is so uncomfortable. This whole meeting seems like it should be with you, Lucy. You're the one with experience in this sort of thing."

"Yes, you're right, Ben. But there's one reason it has to be your dad and not me."

Perplexed, he asked, "And what's that?"

Lucy looked down the drive where Cal had just driven and said, "Patricia doesn't want to get in bed with me."

* * *

Ben left to join the rangers in the far pasture. Lucy didn't care about what they did; she was only thinking of Cal. Was this how he felt every time she was in danger and he couldn't do anything to help? Probably. What had she put him through all those times? She would ask for his forgiveness and promise never to leave his world again. Then she prayed for his safety and the safety of everyone involved in this operation.

* * *

When Cal arrived at the hotel, the valet parked his car while he went inside. Patricia hadn't come down yet, obviously. The maître d' checked his reservation and showed him to a table by a window. He saw Patricia come through the door into the restaurant. As she came toward him, he thought she was a very striking woman but with a rather dour expression. There was no light in her eyes, or maybe he was just used to looking at Lucy's. The dress she was wearing left very little to the imagination. He rose and helped her with her chair.

"It's nice to see you again, Patricia," he lied.

She flashed a provocative smile and said, "Yes, I thought we might never get the chance to meet away from the ranch. You ignored my phone calls for a long time."

"I'm sorry about that. Everyone at the ranch was having difficulty with their phones for a couple of weeks. I think a tower was out of commission or something."

"Mmm, well it doesn't matter now, because here we are. Right?"

"Right. So are you still interested in leasing the ranch house on my other property?"

"No, I don't believe it would be a good fit for me, and I was a bit worried about your wife when she met me with a rifle in her hands," she laughed.

"Yes, Lucy is quite the marksman. She had been out practicing that morning."

They continued the non-important conversation all through dinner. Cal could hardly eat his meal. Every morsel seemed to stick in his throat, making it difficult to swallow.

Finally, as they were having an after-dinner drink, Patricia got down to business.

"You're probably wondering why I wanted to meet you, Cal. There are several reasons. One of them is, of course, because I am extremely attracted to you and hope you feel the same way about me. The other reasons are strictly business related. I'm associated with a large organization, and I think you would be the perfect complement to that organization. We are in need of an experienced cattleman. You know, one who knows how to recognize the best breeds of cattle and can calculate rates of gain and ratios in his head."

"You flatter me, Patricia. I'm not sure I could do all that. What's the name of your organization, if you don't mind me asking?"

She hesitated for a minute, and then narrowed her eyes as though she were assessing how far she could trust him. "It's called Carmion. Ever heard of it?"

"I don't believe so. Exactly what do you do, and how would I be involved? Would I have to move from the ranch?"

"Possibly, in the future you would have to move, but not right now. There's a lot of money to be made, Cal. I like you, and I know I'm going out on a limb by trusting you, but I think I can tell you more when we go to my room later. Let's dance now, shall we?"

Cal's thoughts were spinning. *Go to her room?* That was not part of the deal. He would rather they take every head of cattle on the ranch and the ranch too, before he would do that.

As they danced, she leaned into him and rested her head on his chest.

"Why don't you tell me a little more about your proposal now so when we get to your room, we don't have to waste time talking?" He couldn't believe he had just said that.

She smiled up at him. "I like the way you think, Cal. Okay, here it is. We are a group of investors that want to develop thousands of acres of ranch land into housing communities. Most of the ranch owners are so stubborn about their land and heritage and all that crap that they won't consider selling no matter how high the offered price is, so we try to persuade them to sell, one way or another. We either take away their livelihood by rustling their herds or we ruin their markets or a few times we have burned barns. Really, we will do anything that makes them willing to sell to us."

Cal saw the ranger approaching from behind Patricia.

"Ms. Kitson, you are under arrest. I can cuff you here or out front. It's your choice."

She looked at Cal, eyes blazing. "I cannot believe this. It will be my word against yours in court." The ranger advised her of her rights and then told her, "I wouldn't bet on that, ma'am. We have your recorded admission of guilt, and it will stand up in court." Patricia called Cal every name she could think of, and that was a lot of them.

A second ranger showed up and told Cal the state police had arrested the drivers of the trucks, and his calves were being returned to his ranch at that very minute.

Cal walked outside, feeling like his knees were going to buckle under him. He let the ranger take the recording device and had the valet retrieve his car. As he drove home, all he could smell was Patricia's perfume stuck to his shirt. He contemplated taking it off and throwing it out the window, but realized he might have a hard time explaining to Lucy how he came home with no shirt. Lucy…all he wanted right now was to be in her arms, safe and sound.

* * *

When Lucy heard the car pull in, she met him at the door. "I was worried about you. Let me see … no bullet holes, huh?"

"Nope, no bullet holes but I'm going to take a shower right now and throw this shirt away. I have to get the smell of her perfume off me."

"Okay. Can I ask how close you two were that her perfume is on your shirt?"

"No, don't ask. Why don't you pour a glass of wine for each of us? We can drink it when I get out of the shower, and I'll tell you all about my evening."

Even with the water running full force, he heard the door open. "Lucy?"

"Yes, it's me. I brought the wine in here. I thought maybe we could drink it while we showered, Cowboy." With that, she pulled the shower curtain aside and stepped in with him, handing him a glass of wine.

* * *

After Cal gave her a detailed description of the evening, neither one of them could go to sleep. They lay awake and talked for the entire night.

Lucy moved closer to him so he could put his arm around her. "Cal, I was worried about you tonight. It made me realize how you must have felt when I put myself in a dangerous situation. I'm sorry for doing that to you. I promise it won't happen again."

"Please tell me you weren't concerned about me being with Patricia."

"No, I wasn't worried about her...jealous, maybe, but not worried. I was frightened for your safety. These people weren't playing; they're part of a dangerous organization."

"We don't have to think about them anymore, Sweetheart. I was told it is an airtight case against them. They will all be sentenced for a very long time."

"With the exception of Caleb. No one knows where he is, right?" Lucy asked.

Cal nodded, "Right. They haven't found him yet, but I'm sure they will."

"Mmmm, I hope they do," Lucy said aloud. To herself she thought, *We haven't seen the last of him. He'll resurface. I would bet any amount of money on it.*

* * *

"Cal, do you think if we'd met when we were young, we would have been attracted to each other?"

Cal laughed at her, "Probably not. I wasn't nearly as handsome then as I am today. Although I do believe we met once when I was here for a few weeks during the summer."

"Really? Are you sure? I certainly would remember meeting you."

"I was already in college so you were probably getting ready to start your first year of college. The mailman mistakenly delivered a package to my Dad's house that was addressed to your grandmother. When I came in from working on fences, Dad asked me to take it to your house. When I rode up, you were standing on the porch. I said…"

Lucy interrupted him, "Delivery by Pony Express."

"Yes, that's right. See? We did meet, sort of. I remember thinking you were a very pretty girl, but since I was leaving in a few days, I didn't consider asking you out."

"Cal, did you date anyone after Kathy died?"

"I had a couple of arranged dates, because some friends thought I needed to circulate again. I didn't really enjoy myself. The women were nice, but not one of them asked me to kiss her when I took her home," he teased.

Lucy laughed, "Well, it's a good thing this woman asked you or you wouldn't have asked her out again."

"Yes, I would have. I have no explanation for it, but I knew the minute I saw you in that karaoke club we were going to be more than friends, and when you kissed me like you did, I was going to try my best to win your heart. How about you? Did you date after John died?"

"No. I was too exhausted from working two jobs and trying to make ends meet for the kids. Even though we had insurance, the medical bills were astronomical. I didn't want to use the money from John's trust, and I held out as long as I could. I would go to the community food bank to get extra food. It was humiliating to me, but some weeks, it was all we had to eat. I would have done anything for Paul and Victoria, including swallowing my pride. Maybe that's why when my business was doing well, I tried to pay my employees a higher-than-average wage. I never wanted to think they were struggling to feed their children. I did have dinner with business acquaintances occasionally, but most of them were either very boring or they wanted to go to bed after dinner. I guess I did get lonely at some point, and that's when Derek came into my life. I can honestly say I never loved him but he was a 'warm body' for a short time." Lucy continued, "I've never been accused of being shy, but I surprised myself when I asked you to kiss me that first night. I knew, just like you did, that somehow, we were going to be together forever."

Cal put his arms around her. "It seems we were waiting for each other, Lucy."

"Is your financial advisor in Magnolia or Cypress?" Lucy asked, changing the subject once more.

"He's in Cypress, only two doors from Jerry's office. Why?"

"I want to switch my accounts from the office in Illinois to a local office. I know everything is done online, but I like to look at a person across the desk from me when I'm discussing money."

Cal looked at her and asked, "Are you planning big changes? What money are you talking about?"

"All of it, Cal. You know my house in Batavia sold, plus I own two other business properties in downtown Batavia which are for sale. I have money in various places and accounts, and I want it all in one place. I want to combine it with your accounts, if that's okay with you."

"You don't have to do that, Lucy. We can keep everything separate. And...are you sure this is something you want to discuss at 3 in the morning?"

"It's the perfect time. After all, if we disagree about something, we can settle it while we are lying close to each other. Right?"

Cal smiled at her, "Sounds like logical reasoning to me. So let's talk."

"I meant what I said to you in our wedding vows. Everything I have is yours. I don't want it to be 'your money' and 'my money.' I think it should be 'our money' and 'our children' and 'our grandchildren.' I consider Ben a son just like Paul. Is that some kind of warped thinking?"

"No, it's not warped at all…unusual for people in our situation, probably, but it makes me love you even more, if that's remotely possible."

"Listen, Cal, I have more than enough resources to last while I'm alive and long after I die. God blessed my business and my investments, although I don't know why when I wanted nothing to do with him. I would like to do whatever it takes to combine the two ranches, if that's what you decide to do. My financial advisor and my attorney nearly had apoplexy when I refused to have a pre-nuptial agreement signed. I knew there was no need for one. We can still have our own checking accounts if that makes things easier, but I don't like being separate from you in any way, not monetarily and definitely not physically," she said as she snuggled closer.

"I meant what I said on our wedding day, also, Lucy. Absolutely everything I have is yours, and I like the idea of it being combined to be 'ours' instead of 'yours' and 'mine.' I think it will save a lot of concerns in our wills, also. Do you think we could ask God to take us both home at exactly the same time so neither one of us will be left without the other?"

"We can certainly ask although it only happens like that in the movies, I think. Right now, I need you to hold me tight, Cal."

"If I hold you any tighter, I'll crack your ribs," he laughed.

"No you won't," Lucy said, shaking her head. "I don't break easily, but I need your arms around me. It gives me security and strength and assures me that you will always be there, holding me, keeping me safe."

"I will never let you go, Lucy Mae. You are my very life."

Cal glanced at the clock. "In an hour it will be time to get up. Do you want to try to sleep for at least a little bit?"

"I won't fall asleep. Just continue to hold me like this, Cowboy."

Chapter 19

"HELLO, IS THIS MRS. WATKINS?" Lucy asked when Phoebe answered her phone.

"Why yes, it is. Who is calling, please?" Phoebe could hardly talk without laughing. "Lucy, I have been missing you so badly. You will never know."

"I cannot believe you eloped to Vegas without telling me. My feelings are hurt," Lucy teased. "Seriously, we have to talk. I am going to the Frasier ranch house to clean before Paul and Lynne come to see it. Would you like to come and keep me company? No cleaning required, just sit and talk to me."

"I would love to, but I have no car until Jerry and I go car shopping this weekend. Could you come and get me?"

"Yes, of course. I'll pick you up at 8 o'clock tomorrow morning. I want to hear everything that happened between the time Cal and I left your house and right now. Well, maybe not *every* single thing, but you know..." Lucy laughed. "And I'll tell you about the rustling ring and Cal's date with a woman who was involved."

"What?" Phoebe yelled into the phone. "I won't be able to sleep tonight waiting to hear *that* story."

Lucy laughed, "You're a newlywed. You're not supposed to be sleeping anyway."

"I'll see you at 8, Lucy."

Lucy spent the rest of the morning cleaning the guest house situated behind the main ranch house on the Benson ranch. Paul and Lynne and the kids could stay there when they came for Cal's birthday. She put clean sheets on the beds and made sure the refrigerator was clean so she could stock it with food later, closer to the date they would arrive. She really hoped they would decide to move to the house on the Frasier ranch. It would be nice to have them close. Then, as Cal said, 'All of our family would be close.' She considered how fortunate she was to have all five of her and Cal's children feel like family to her. In the beginning, she wasn't sure that would ever transpire. She sat on the couch and dialed Samantha's number.

"Hi Samantha. I wondered if you and the children would like to stay overnight on the Fourth, since you have the farthest drive and I don't want you to drive home alone late at night."

"Thank you, Lucy. I will ask Sean what he wants to do. He said he would like to come."

"Perfect. I'll make sure the rooms above the great room are ready in case you decide to stay…and Samantha, I'm happy Sean is coming," she added.

Her next phone call was to Simon. She left a message. "Simon, I want you and Chloe to come for a cookout on the Fourth. We'll celebrate Cal's birthday, too. No gifts, please. Just come and join us for food, fun, and fireworks. My son and his family will be here, so you can meet the little girl you flew me to see in Illinois when she was in the hospital. Hope to see you. Bye."

She finished the cleaning and went home to make a few more calls. Cal said he would be free to meet the financial advisor later in the afternoon, so she showered and got dressed. While she waited for Cal, she called Allen, the young man in Illinois who had a son with autism. They talked for a long time. His son was 13 years old and doing well in school. He gave Lucy the names of some organizations that might help with information. Then he spoke from his heart.

"When parents first hear the word 'autism,' it immediately brings all sorts of visions to mind, most of which are not accurate, but it happens anyway. Then they go through the stages of grief: they're angry that their child won't be all they hoped for, they are sad and feel sorry for themselves, they go through denial, telling themselves the doctors must be wrong and then hope that there will be some miracle cure…and finally, acceptance. You can't move on until you accept the fact your child may be different but not defective. There are many types of therapies available that can improve skills and behaviors and learning. In fact, one of the therapies used is horseback riding. Don't you live on a ranch with horses?"

"Yes, I do. But I don't know what to do. Is there a place I can go to learn simple riding therapy skills?" Lucy asked.

"I hate to use this cliché answer, but Google it. I'm certain there are riding therapy providers in your area. Visit them and ask for the basics so you can help your grandson. If your daughter-in-law will go with you, take her to some of the therapy schools. Many have therapy dogs, also. We don't have one, but I know a family that does, and it has helped their child immensely. If he isn't speaking, you can use some basic sign language to start with so he can communicate the things he wants. Often, the child feels trapped because of their inability to communicate. One of the tough things about autism is it is an entire spectrum of abilities and disabilities. Very few children are exactly the same. There is so much more I could tell you but you probably have enough for one day. Please call me any time you have a question. You were very good to us when I worked for you, Louisa, and I will do anything I can to help."

"Thank you, Allen. I appreciate your time and sharing your experiences. I'm certain you will be hearing from me again," she laughed. "I will let you know how much information I accumulate."

When she and Cal were on their way to Cypress, she told him about the call to Allen. "I really want to talk to Jackie and Gary about all of this, but I think I should go to the library for more information and visit a riding therapy school first. What are your thoughts about the whole thing? Maybe you should speak to her instead of me."

Cal looked at her and smiled that smile she loved. "I think you are the most caring person I know, Lucy. You never do anything halfway, do you?"

"Gabe is a *whole* little boy; he doesn't deserve me doing anything halfway. I want Jackie and Gary to have some peace about this and about the new baby, too. I have been praying about it and how to proceed without being the interfering mother-in-law."

* * *

The man who was familiar with Cal's accounts, John Lincoln, was out of town, so they were ushered into the office of a young man Cal didn't know. When they were seated and Cal had introduced Lucy, he asked what he could do for them.

Cal explained, "We would like to move my wife's assets here from Illinois and then combine them with mine, so they are all in one account."

"I don't mean to imply anything, but do you really think that's a good idea, Mr. Frasier? You don't have a pre-nuptial agreement, I see, and I don't usually advise clients to put both names on their accounts. You have substantial investments that you should probably keep separate."

Cal saw the look on Lucy's face and knew he needed to head off the train wreck that was coming. "Perhaps you would like to peruse my wife's information before you say anything else you might regret," he cautioned the young man.

Lucy handed him the envelope containing her information. He looked at it for a bit, then let out a low whistle and looked at Lucy as if he had not seen her previously. He cleared his throat and said, "Well, I see you have a very nice portfolio of investments, Mrs. Frasier. I must say, the bottom line of your worth is definitely impressive."

Lucy turned to Cal and gave him a look that said, *"I'm going to knock that twit right out of his chair."*

Instead she said, "That is actually only part of my net worth. I have some real estate in Illinois, some accounts that are out of the country, and I have a solid amount of cash. Do you still think our assets shouldn't be combined?"

"Oh no, Mrs. Frasier. I think together, you and Mr. Frasier would have a very impressive account balance."

While the account transfers wouldn't produce any income for him, the assets that needed to be sold and turned into cash before purchasing new investments certainly would. Lucy saw the dollar signs spinning around in his head as he calculated his commission. She waited for Cal to say something before she voiced her opinion.

"I think we should think about this for a while. I'll contact John when he gets back and perhaps we can come back to discuss the whole situation." Cal held out his hand for Lucy's envelope, and they left the office.

Lucy looked at Cal and smiled, "I wasn't carrying my revolver, you know…I wasn't going to threaten to shoot him."

Cal chuckled. "From the look on your face, I was afraid you might go over the desk and strangle him instead."

"That thought occurred to me," Lucy replied. "Why can't people do what you ask without always assuming if a female is involved, she can't possibly know what she's talking about or in this case, have any money? It really annoys me."

"I can tell, Sweetheart. Let's go have a sandwich at the Long Branch Café where this whole relationship started."

Their server was Lacey, the young girl who waited on Lucy the first night she came to Cypress, last year.

Lacey looked at Cal, and shyly greeted him. "Hello, Mr. Frasier." Then she cocked her head to one side and looked at Lucy, as though she was trying to remember her, too. Lucy helped her out.

"Lacey, you were my server a year ago when I stopped in here. You told me Cal Frasier was a nice man. Remember? Well, you were right, he is a nice man."

Lacey nodded in recognition. "Yes. I only work here when I'm not in class, but I do remember watching you looking at him. So, I guess you got to meet him, huh?"

Lucy nodded and reached across the table to touch Cal's hand. "I not only met him…I married him."

Chapter 20

PHOEBE WAS READY AND WAITING when Lucy arrived. They hugged and were off to the unoccupied ranch house.

"So…start talking, Phoebe. How did you happen to get married in Las Vegas?"

Phoebe couldn't stop smiling. "It all happened so fast, Lucy. One minute we were in my bedroom where you left us and the next thing I knew we were on a plane to Vegas. You know, you don't need a blood test, or waiting period, or anything except proof of identification and proof of divorce if you were previously married. It's a good thing Jerry is a meticulous record keeper. Even after all these years, he knew exactly where his divorce papers were located and could access them online. We packed enough clothes for a week, and the next thing I knew, I was Mrs. Jerry Watkins."

Lucy looked at her friend and knew she was happy. "Phoebe, I am beyond ecstatic for you and Jerry. I had no idea when I asked you to come to Texas with me to help paint bedrooms at Vicki's house, you would meet someone. And even better, now my best friend lives close to me. God certainly has a way of working things out, doesn't he?"

"Yeah, about that…" Phoebe sighed. "You know I never felt like you did about God. I mean, you knew him and chose to turn away. I never knew him in my entire life, and I didn't want to know a God that would take my son from me. I'm not going to lie and say everything in the 'God department' is lovely, but Jerry and I have agreed to take things slow and I will attend Bible study night at church with him. He understands and is not pushing me."

"That's a good beginning, Phoebe. I feel that I have come full circle and can't imagine my life without God in it. I spend an awful lot of time in prayer, it seems, because there is always some sort of problem I can't find my way through. Seems like there is a new one every day."

"Like going to the jail the other day?"

Lucy laughed. "Are you going to lecture me, too?"

"Nope. Actually, I thought you did the right thing, and I'm not supposed to tell you this, but after Jerry thought about it for a while and then spoke to Mr. Tanner, he admitted you were the catalyst to resolve the situation, hopefully."

"That's nice to know. Now somebody needs to tell Vicki, who is still not speaking to me, I believe."

They entered the house with some trepidation, not knowing for sure what they would find, since the man who leased it had left unexpectedly. It was in surprisingly good shape, overall, but it was dusty and definitely in need of updating in some areas.

"It smells musty and old. I need to get rid of that odor. I want Paul and Lynne to have a good first impression when they see it. I'm not sure where to start, Phoebe."

Phoebe moved to a window and pulled the drapes open. "These need to come down, Lucy, and I think the musty smell is coming from the carpeting."

"Okay," Lucy agreed. "Let's start by going room to room and writing down what each one needs: paint, carpet, or whatever else needs our attention. We'll check to see if the water pressure is good and everything works.

As they made lists, Phoebe observed, "This could be an expensive makeover, Lucy."

"I don't care, Phoebe. Cost isn't important to me at the moment." She continued by telling Phoebe about the meeting yesterday in the broker's office. They were both laughing hysterically by the time she got to the part where Cal got her out of there before she strangled the young man.

Phoebe commented, "Cal must know your facial expressions pretty well."

"Yes, he does. That's one more thing I love about the man. He knows me so well, everything from my moods to my expressions, my thoughts, my sarcasm, my needs. It's like we've known each other forever. I don't know how that happened, but I'm happy it did."

"Jerry and I are remarkably intuitive about each other, too. Maybe it has something to do with age. You reach a time where you can focus on the person you love instead of all the other things we *think* need our attention…like new curtains," she said as she pulled another set open to let the light into the room.

"I think you're right, and as far as money goes, I've been without a dime and now have money. As some comedian said, 'I prefer having it' but it doesn't solve everything. It will buy new carpet and paint, but when Annie was in the hospital in a coma, it couldn't help a bit."

They checked the appliances and cleaned the kitchen and bathrooms. "I think I've come to a decision," Lucy said when they took a break. "I'm not going to find a company that will be able to do all these renovations before they get here. Paul and Lynne are smart enough to be able to look at the house and make a decision. If they decide to move here, they can choose the colors and type of flooring. Then I would have a few months to have it completed. Their lease isn't up until August. I think that's a better idea, don't you?"

"It sounds good to me. Jerry has talked about looking for another place to live, also. He thinks the condo he has is too much 'him' and would like something that would reflect both our tastes. There are so many things to consider. Do I sell my furniture with the house in Illinois or should I move some of it here? Should I sell my car and buy a new one or should I fly back and drive mine down here? I have the business to put on the market, too. It's overwhelming sometimes. Speaking of businesses, the one property you have in downtown Batavia is leased by a sweet young woman who makes and sells jewelry. I think her name is Anna. She shared with me that she would really like to purchase it but doesn't know how to approach you about maybe buying it on contract or something, because she doesn't have the means to finance it."

"Really?" Lucy replied. "I'll give her a call. I'm sure we can work something out that would make us both happy. That will have to wait, though. Right now, I am sinking fast," she laughed. "I have to finish the arrangements for Cal's birthday party, pick up his guitar, and order a cake. I invited Samantha and her family to spend the night after the party, so the upstairs bedrooms have to be cleaned. Paul and Lynne want to check this house, but they are staying in the guest house. Whew."

Phoebe laughed at her. "And you have to get back in good graces with Vicki, and you mentioned you need to learn more about autism? What's up with that?"

Lucy hadn't mentioned Jackie and her thoughts about an abortion to Phoebe. She knew Phoebe had an abortion when Todd was little, and she didn't want to bring up bad memories. Phoebe asked again, so she told her briefly about Jackie and her being pregnant and considering an abortion due to her fear of having another child with autism.

Phoebe's expression clouded for a second, and then quietly, she said, "I never forgave myself for having an abortion. At the time, it seemed like the only way out. I couldn't bear the thought of bringing another child into my nightmare of a world. I always thought if there really was a God, he punished me for that abortion when Todd died."

Lucy put her arms around her friend. "Oh Phoebe, you never told me you thought Todd's death was a punishment. It was an accident caused by an evil man, not because of something you did. God doesn't work that way. Of course, abortion makes him sad, but he forgives us when we ask, just as with any other sin. Does Jerry know you carry this in your heart?"

"No. He knows about the abortion, but not that I think Todd's death was my punishment. We haven't discussed that yet."

Lucy looked at her friend and smiled, "When the time is right, you tell him how you feel. I know he will tell you the same thing I just did. God loves you, Phoebe, please believe that."

Lucy relayed the story of Cal's date with Patricia in Houston. Finally, Lucy stood and said, "Let's close this place up. I'll sweep the front porch, and Paul and Lynne will have to use their imaginations as to what it will look like with updated décor. Hopefully, they will like it, but I can't control their decision."

Together, they picked up the repaired guitar and ordered the cake. They stopped for lunch, and then Lucy took Phoebe home before she stopped to see Vicki.

When Vicki answered the door, Lucy tried to guess what she was thinking but couldn't so she asked instead. "Have you forgiven me yet or am I still persona non grata?"

Vicki managed a smile and invited her inside. "Oh, Mom. No matter how angry I get at you, I can never stay that way. You always catch me off guard with your 'git 'er done' philosophy and actions. I like to plan things and think them through before I take any action. Are you sure I'm your daughter? Maybe I was adopted."

"Believe me, Honey, you are definitely my daughter. I don't know where that 'planning and think-before-you-act' gene came from, though; that must be from your father," she laughed.

"Well, as usual, you did us a favor. We have a mediation meeting with Blake Tanner next week. We're waiting for the adoption agency and the state to be available so this can be over."

Lucy picked up Olivia and snuggled her. "Mmmm, I love that powdery baby smell. Vicki, can I ask a favor? At Cal's birthday party, would you make sure Jackie gets to hold Olivia a lot?"

Vicki looked perplexed but said, "Sure. I can do that. Can I ask why?"

"Let's just say that in this case, a baby may be worth a thousand words."

CHAPTER 21

"GRAAAAMMMMYYYY." Annie came flying in the door with her arms stretched out wide and threw them around Lucy. "I missed you so much."

Lucy picked her up and squeezed her. "I missed you, too, Baby. Your legs are getting so long. Pretty soon I won't be able to pick you up any longer. Where's the rest of your family?"

"They're coming. They stopped to talk to Grandpa Cal, but I wanted to see you first."

Lucy smiled at her curly-haired little girl. She had such a soft spot in her heart for Annie. Her pink cowboy hat fell off when she jumped into Lucy's arms. She stood now and retrieved it and went back out to show Cal that she remembered to bring it. Lucy followed her outside.

Paul saw her first and gave her a big hug, and then Lynne and Jarrod joined them. "It's good to have you here," Lucy told them. "Let's get your bags into the guest house, and then we can have time for a visit."

Everyone grabbed a bag or suitcase and took them around to the guest house. With Ben's help, they made it in one trip. Paul shook his head at the pile of luggage. "Girls…I don't know how they can need so much stuff for just a few days. I feel like Lynne and Annie brought everything they own, while Jarrod and I threw a couple of changes of clothes into a bag, and we were done."

"Get used to it, Paul," Ben told him. "I grew up with two sisters, and it was always that way."

Jarrod took Cal's hand on the way back to the main house. "Dad says we might move here, Grandpa. Is there room for us?"

"It wouldn't be in this house, Jarrod. There is another house on our other ranch, and it has plenty of room for your family. It is a big house."

"Could I have my own horse?"

Cal didn't want to get Jarrod's hopes up if they decided against moving there. "Before I answer that, Jarrod, let's let your mom and dad look at it and talk about it, okay? Moving a family is a big deal. You know how it was when you moved from your house in Illinois to Oklahoma. Grown-ups have to think about a lot of things before they make a decision like that. But I'll make sure you get to ride while you're here, okay?"

That seemed to satisfy Jarrod for the time being.

They all had a glass of lemonade. "I'm happy you decided to come a few days early. That will give you time to look at the house tomorrow, and we get to visit with you alone for a bit."

Lynne asked, "Would it be possible to look at the house today? I'm so excited about the prospect of living close to family again; I can hardly wait to see it!"

"Sure, that's fine," Cal said. "I thought perhaps you were tired from your trip. Let's go. Follow us over there."

Cal and Lucy gave them the tour of the house. Lucy explained the rooms would be painted and new flooring put down, but she would let them choose the colors they wanted.

"Are you trying to influence our decision, Mom?" Paul teased her.

"No, not at all," Lucy said. Then she looked at Cal and confessed, "Well, yeah, I really am."

Cal told Paul, "Now you know the truth. We would like you to be here but understand if it isn't feasible. Don't we, Lucy?"

Paul watched his mom and Cal together. She seemed much softer, if that was the right word, and happier than he had ever seen her in his entire life. He wouldn't have believed she could give up her "mover and shaker" lifestyle to be Cal's wife. He was happy for them.

"Are we going to have fireworks, Grammy?" Annie asked as she skipped around the large living room.

"You bet we are, Annie. What would the Fourth of July be without some fireworks? Your Uncle Ben was in charge of buying them, so I don't know what he has, but I'm sure they will be beautiful."

* * *

After dinner, Paul and Lynne left to put their things away in the guest house, while Cal took Jarrod and Annie for short rides on the ATVs down the front drive and partway to the road. When the mosquitoes came out with a vengeance, the kids went to their house to have baths and get ready for bed.

* * *

"Cal, I want to give you your birthday gift now instead of at the party. Is that okay? Tomorrow is really your birthday, anyway," Lucy said.

He put his arm around her and whispered, "Your kind of gift would most definitely be better here than at the party."

"Okay, Cowboy, we're not talking about that kind of gift. I have an actual present for you." She asked him to sit down and close his eyes while she went to get it from its hiding place. "I hope you like it, Cal. Open your eyes."

He took the guitar out of the new case and caressed it lovingly. "Is this really my old guitar?" he asked.

"It is. Refurbished, if you will, but still the original."

Cal strummed it and then softly started to sing the song he sang to her at the hotel—"I Want to Be Your Man."

Lucy sat on the floor and listened to him as he played several songs. When he stopped and put it back in the case, she took his hand and said, "Now about that other present..."

* * *

The next two days were a blur as everything was prepared for the party. Paul and Lynne and the kids went to visit Vicki and David for a day. Ben was ready to set the fireworks up behind the house in a large open area. It had been the runway for Lucy's father's plane at one time. The earth was like cement, and grass had never grown there. There were a few times when Simon had used it as a runway for his plane. Ben made sure there was a source of water in case a stray spark made it off the runway area.

Lucy hoped she had thought of everything but no doubt had forgotten some detail. This would be the first time the entire family was together since the wedding and the first birthday she and Cal had celebrated together.

She had arranged for the ranch cook, Dolores, and her husband, Sam, to do the grilling and prepare the food. There were games for the children to play. Paul helped Cal set up tables in the side yard. The cake was ready, and they were going to use the old-fashioned hand-cranked ice cream makers for the ice cream.

Samantha and Sean were the first to arrive. Paul and Lynne and Ben and Candy were already there, of course. Jackie and Gary and David and Vicki drove up the drive at the same time. Pandemonium was the only word Lucy could think of to describe the scene in front of her, and she loved it. Annie and Amy paired up, and Jarrod, Doug, and Devon found things to do. Bethany was a bit overwhelmed by it all, and Gabe stayed close to Gary, although he would go with Cal. Vicki asked Jackie to hold Olivia while she helped Bethany with a game the girls were playing. Candy was miserable, but Ben took good care of her. He made her as comfortable as was possible. The other adult guests arrived and wished Cal a happy birthday. Simon asked where Annie was. When Lynne found her, Simon crouched down to her level and told her he was the one who promised her a ride in his plane when her leg was healed.

"If it's okay with your parents, I would like to keep that promise tomorrow." After he saw the look of disappointment on the other children's faces, he asked if he could take all four of the older ones, providing a parent rode along. Amy did not want to go, so Sean and Ben volunteered to accompany the other three children.

Everyone ate until they were stuffed. Ben fixed a plate for Candy who was laughing about the fact she had her own table and could set a plate on her protruding belly. Cal brought his guitar out. He sat Gabe next to him and played songs for the kids. They sang and danced around while the parents took pictures. Jackie told Cal, "I remember when you used to play for us, Dad. Can you still play 'Old McDonald Had a Farm?'"

"Of course I can…I think," he answered. Gabe smiled but wouldn't leave Cal's side.

"I have another song to play, but this one is for Lucy," Cal explained. He sang and played "The Yellow Rose of Texas" for her as she sat by him.

"You're going to make me cry, Cowboy," she told him.

* * *

After the cake and ice cream was devoured, it was time for fireworks. Lucy had an idea for Gabe as she knew the noise would be horrific for him. She brought her sound inhibitors out and handed them to Cal. "Perhaps you can convince him to wear them, although they may be more than he can handle, too."

Cal put them on his own head and showed Gabe. Then he attempted to put them on Gabe's head. Finally, he handed them to him and let him play with them for a while and try to put them on himself. Gabe seemed to be okay with that and liked the fireworks now that he didn't have to hear the noise. Gary and Jackie looked on as he sat on Cal's lap watching the pretty colors. Cal looked at Lucy over Gabe's head and nodded and smiled at her idea.

When the food and games were put away, everyone gathered inside the house for a cup of coffee and more cake if they wanted it.

Cal and Lucy remained on the porch looking out over the drive with their arms around each other's waist. "Happy birthday, Cal," she whispered.

"I have an idea, Lucy. Let's go riding tomorrow just like we did that first time, but with no rattlesnakes, okay? We can take a lunch with us, maybe even white wine with collapsible cups," he chuckled remembering their first lunch. "These children of ours can take care of themselves for a day. The kids are going with Simon, and Paul and Lynne are staying a few more days. I want to spend the day with you, alone."

He turned her to face him and then kissed her long and passionately.

Inside the house, Annie said, "Hey, Grammy is kissing Grandpa again."

Everyone turned to look out the window.

"Should I be embarrassed by my mother?" Vicki laughed.

Samantha spoke up and said quietly, while looking at Sean, "No, not at all. I fervently pray my husband and I are that much in love when we are that age."

Chapter 22

CAL SADDLED CUTTER AND HARMONY while Lucy packed leftovers into a small soft-sided cooler. They slipped out of the house while everyone was still asleep. Jackie, Gary, and Gabe and Vicki, David, and the children had gone home last night after the party. Samantha and Sean, Amy and Doug stayed in the guestrooms upstairs.

"I feel like we're doing something we shouldn't, sneaking away like this," Lucy laughed.

"We told all of them we would be gone this morning, so they shouldn't be surprised when they wake up. I'm sure they can all find something for breakfast," Cal assured her.

They mounted and left the house and yard behind. Cal led the way along a narrow trail that led to a large pasture where they could ride next to each other.

"I think Samantha and Sean may have worked through their problems. They certainly looked happy together last night," Lucy commented.

"You're right," Cal agreed. "I noticed she asked Sean's opinion about several things, too, instead of making all the decisions, like she used to do."

"I asked Vicki to make sure Jackie held Olivia while they were there. I thought that sweet baby might influence her decision about the baby she's carrying. I don't know if it helped, but I thought it was worth a shot."

"You know, Lucy, I love that little Gabriel so much. I hope the horse-riding therapy might help him some."

Lucy smiled, "He has certainly attached himself to you, Cal. You may be the one to help him the most. I love seeing him with you."

"Do you think Paul and Lynne are going to agree to move into the other house?" Cal asked.

"I don't know. I was trying to get a feel for their answer, without asking outright, but I wasn't making any headway. I guess we'll know in a few days, before they leave. I hope they do. I think Lynne would move in tomorrow, but Paul is taking his time to think it through. Where did these kids come from?" Lucy asked. "Vicki said the same thing a few days ago, when she was chastising me for being a *forge-ahead* kind of person. She likes to plan and organize; it must be their dad's genes, because it certainly didn't come from me," she laughed.

Cal had to hold Cutter back as he wanted to stretch out and get some exercise. "Come on, let's go," Lucy told him. They both let the horses have free rein and covered the expanse of the large pasture in record time.

Lucy patted Harmony's neck. "It's okay Baby. Cutter's legs are a lot longer than yours."

They dismounted and walked for a while. "It's going to be really hot soon, Cal. Do you think we should find some shade, for them and for us?"

"Let's go to the next pasture and then over to the bluffs. There's a windmill there for fresh water and trees for shade. We can eat lunch and take a break," Cal suggested.

Lucy noticed some tire tracks and asked, "Is this the pasture they chose to take the calves?"

"Yes. Then they released them here, too. We should probably keep our eyes open for a stray or two. They might not have rounded all of them up after their wild night. Ben said they were all pretty spooked."

Lucy spread the blanket out, and they ate their lunch in the shade of a line of trees while the horses grazed nearby. She removed her boots and hat and wiped the sweat off her face. Cal sat behind her and kissed the back of her neck as he had done the first time they went riding. Lucy turned to him and after a long, loving kiss, she said, "Cal, I would love to sit here all day, but I have to say, this ground is too darned hard."

He laughed at her and agreed. "I think we're spoiled…or old."

"Speak for yourself, okay? I refuse to be old; spoiled, yes, but not old."

They both looked up as they heard the noise of a small plane engine. It was Simon with the children. He came close enough for the kids to wave at them.

Cal shook his head. "It just proves you can't get away from people no matter how far you go."

They rode for a while longer through the scrub trees that were very dense. When they came out on the other side, Lucy told him, "I must have picked up a piece of dirt or a pebble in my boot when I took it off at lunch. I need to get it out, it's bothering me." She sat down, removed her revolver from her boot and then took the boot off. She was going to check the time when she discovered she didn't have her phone in her pocket.

"Cal, could you please walk back a little way through the trees and see if I dropped it on the way? I don't care about the phone, but I hate to lose all the contacts and information that's in it."

Cal led Cutter back the way they had just come, through the dense brush, looking for her phone as he walked. Suddenly, he heard a man's voice coming from the direction where he just left

Lucy. He stood still so he wouldn't make any noise and listened. He recognized that voice. It was Caleb Kitson.

Lucy heard a noise and looked up. She was looking directly at Caleb.

"Well, well, if it isn't the rancher's wife. You and I have some unfinished business, I believe." He had his gun in his hand this time and started to unbuckle his belt with his other hand. Lucy felt for her gun, but he noticed. "Not this time, Sweetheart. Throw that pistol over here."

She hesitated, but when he pointed the gun at her head, she threw the pistol at his feet.

Where was Cal? He couldn't have gone that far looking for her phone, could he?

"You might as well save yourself the trouble of taking your belt off, because it isn't going to happen, I can tell you," she said with more bravado than she felt.

"Choose for yourself, Ms. Frasier. We can have a nice little playtime, or I can shoot you right here. That should punish your husband for all the grief he's caused me."

"I'll choose being shot over spending any time with you, Caleb."

"Have it your way, but you're missing out on a good time." He aimed his gun directly at her head but before he could pull the trigger, she heard a thunderous explosion, and Caleb fell backward. As he fell, his arm came up in an arc and his reflexes pulled the trigger, which caused another explosion.

"Cal, thank God you came back," Lucy said as she put her boot back on and retrieved her revolver. "Cal? Come out here. Caleb is not a threat any longer. You have a very good aim."

"Cal? Where are you?" She kicked Caleb's gun out of his reach in case he was still breathing. Then she went to look for her husband.

She found him…stretched out on the ground with a blood stain covering the front of his shirt. The wild shot from Caleb's gun had found Cal.

"No, no, no. Dear God, please, no. Don't let him die."

Think, Lucy, think. You have to stop the blood. Find the phone. Get some help.

She didn't have time to find her phone. She pulled Cal's from his pocket and called Ben. *Please let him answer, God. Please.*

"Hello, Dad?" Ben said.

"Ben. Listen to me. Your dad's been shot. Where are you and Simon right now?"

"What? Lucy, you're not making any sense. What do you mean, Dad's been shot? We're just landing at Hobby with the kids."

"Please ask Simon if his friend's helicopter is there. Don't ask questions, just do it. Tell him we are through the scrub, just a few yards away from where he saw us when he flew over. Your dad is too heavy for me to get him onto Cutter, and he wouldn't make it to ride out of here anyway. I have to go. Get that helicopter here."

Lucy continued to talk to Cal. "Keep looking at me, Sweetheart. Don't close your eyes. Come on. Breathe, but don't try to talk."

She had to stop the flow of blood. What herbs did Grandpa tell her would do that? Frostweed and yarrow. She didn't remember what frostweed looked like but she would find some yarrow. It grew in the hot arid places. She searched until she found some plants. She stripped the leaves off and wadded them up. How was she going to keep them on the wound? She needed a bandage. Lucy took Cal's knife off his belt and cut a hole in the top of her shirtsleeve. She put her fingers in the hole and ripped the sleeve off. Then she did the same to the other one and tied them together. Would they go around him? No.

"Oh, Honey, why do you have such a big chest?"

She cut a hole in one of Cal's sleeves and carefully tore it out too. Now, tied together, the three sleeves would go around him. She opened his shirt, placed the yarrow leaves on the wound and tied the makeshift bandage tightly around him to hold it in place.

"Look at me, Cal. Don't talk. Breathe. We're going to get out of here, I promise." Blood- tinged saliva was bubbling out of his mouth with every breath he took. When he closed his eyes, Lucy patted his face to force him to open them again. She felt for his pulse; it was thready but still beating, thank God. She slid her hand under his back. She couldn't feel any wound where the bullet had exited so it had to be lodged inside somewhere. From the trouble he was having breathing, she would guess it was in his lung. *Where are you, Simon?*

* * *

Simon heard Ben's part of the conversation but didn't want to scare the children. As he landed, he saw his friend's helicopter was at the field. Now to get it in the air and find Cal and Lucy. He would explain to his friend later.

Ben unloaded the kids and asked Paul, who was waiting to pick them up, to take them home. He briefly told him what he knew, which wasn't much, beyond the fact that Cal had been shot.

Sean said, "I'm going along. You'll need help to lift him in there. Your dad is a big man."

Simon waited for the two men to get in. Ben asked Sean, "You know how to ride, don't you, Sean?"

"Yes. I do. You want me to bring the horses back?"

"Yes, please. I don't know what we'll find when we get there, but we can't leave the horses out there." Ben turned to Simon. "How do you know how to fly this thing, Simon, and do you keep a key to it?"

"I flew helicopters when I was in the service. I've always renewed my license. I guess that was a 'God thing' huh? And helicopters don't require a key."

Ben had another thought, "Are you going to be able to land at a hospital if you're not one of their medical helicopters?"

"Yes. I'll tell them I have a critically injured patient on board, and they'll make a place for me to land on the grass or in the parking lot. We'll have to get him to Houston, though. Not the local hospital."

Ben didn't know Simon had flown helicopters in the service. He wondered how Lucy knew that.

* * *

"Keep looking at me, Honey. Come on, please. I know it's hard to breathe, but you have to try. Don't talk. Save your energy."

Finally, after what seemed like an eternity, Lucy heard the 'whump, whump, whump' of the helicopter blades. "Thank you, God," she said aloud.

Simon set it down as close to them as he could. Ben and Sean jumped out. They lifted Cal carefully and placed him on the floor of the helicopter. Then they went back to pick up Caleb.

Lucy turned and said, "He's not coming along. Let him die."

Ben told her, "Lucy. We can't let a man die. He's still breathing."

She started to reach for her gun. "I can take care of that and his breathing," she said with no emotion.

Ben grabbed her gun and shoved her into the helicopter. "Get in there. You're wasting precious time."

When Ben was inside, Simon took off. Sean gathered up Cal's hat and Lucy's hat, the knife she used, Cal's gun, the other man's gun, and all three horses. He mounted Cutter and led the other two. As he watched the helicopter become a speck in the distance, he prayed aloud for Cal. "I know you don't hear from me as much as you would like, Lord, but please take care of Cal. He is a God-fearing man and the patriarch of this family. Please don't let him die."

Lucy continued to talk to Cal, urging him to keep breathing and to keep his eyes open.

At one point, Ben heard her say to the other man lying on the floor, "If Cal dies and you live, I guarantee you will wish Ben had let me shoot you."

Chapter 23

BEFORE THEY REACHED Hermann Memorial Hospital, Simon radioed ahead and let them know he had a medical emergency, with two critically injured individuals on board, both with gunshot wounds.

He was advised of the location where he could land. Trauma teams would be waiting for them. He also called his friend to assure him no one had stolen his helicopter.

Lucy continued to urge Cal to keep his eyes open, but his breathing was becoming more and more labored. He looked at her with eyes full of fear and with great difficulty he managed to say "Lucy" before he lost consciousness.

"Cal, open your eyes, please." *God, do not let him die, please.*

Simon landed, and the trauma teams immediately loaded both men onto gurneys and wheeled them inside. Lucy and Ben followed as far as they could. Simon came in long enough to tell them he would be back later but needed to return the helicopter to Hobby.

Ben called Candy to tell her where he was, although he was sure Paul had made it home by now and everyone knew where they were. He called Samantha to tell her where Sean was, in case he hadn't made it back to the ranch yet. She answered her phone and said she had Jackie with her, and they were on their way to the hospital.

Lucy felt as though she was living in a dream world that had turned into a nightmare. Her hands and shirt were covered in Cal's blood, and her hair was clinging to her face in wet strands. There were no tears but she felt as though she had just died when they wheeled him through the doors and she couldn't follow.

Ben sat next to her, neither one saying anything. Finally, he asked, "Lucy, who was the other man?"

She answered in a dull, monotone voice, barely above a whisper, "Caleb Kitson, grandson of the original Double K owner."

She put her head in her hands and prayed. Ben put his hand on her back to let her know he was still there. Samantha and Jackie arrived, and Ben took them out into the hallway.

"What happened, Ben?"

"Who would want to shoot Dad?"

He briefly explained what he knew, which wasn't much. He knew the name of the man who shot Cal but none of the surrounding circumstances, and Lucy wasn't talking at the moment.

Jerry and Phoebe arrived, too. Lynne had called them. Phoebe knelt in front of Lucy's chair. She pushed the loose strands of hair back and tucked them behind Lucy's ears. "Come on, Honey, let's get you something to drink."

Lucy shook her head. "No, I'm not leaving this room."

Jerry removed his jacket and placed it around Lucy's shoulders. Her bare arms looked cold.

Phoebe asked, "Can I get a warm towel and wash the blood off your face and hands?"

Lucy looked at her hands, then curled them into fists and held them against her chest. "No," she said emphatically. "This blood is all I have of Cal at the moment. You can't wash that off."

Jerry shook his head at Phoebe to say, "Let it go...she needs that right now."

After what seemed like an interminable time, a doctor emerged through the double doors.

He was a rather short man with a rotund middle who was blunt and to the point. "Are one of you ladies the wife of the big guy with the gunshot wound?"

Ben helped Lucy stand up and told him, "She's his wife. I'm his son, and these are his daughters." He indicated Samantha and Jackie.

With a bit of a smile, the doctor asked, "And who is the botanist?"

"I'm afraid I don't know what you're talking about," Ben answered him.

"Who put the poultice of leaves on the wound to keep it from bleeding?"

Lucy looked at him and whispered, "I did."

"Who taught you what plant to use and what was it, exactly?"

"My Grandpa did, and it was yarrow. He said they used it in the wars a long time ago to stop the soldiers from bleeding to death."

"Well, your grandfather was a smart man. You saved your husband's life. He has a bullet lodged in his lung. The good news is that it is operable. Many times, we can leave a bullet in the lung, but not in this case. In all likelihood, we will have to remove a lobe of his lung. Don't worry; we can all live with a lobe removed. My biggest concern right now is his loss of blood and his oxygen levels. He will need a transfusion, for sure. I never make promises, but I'm going to try my best to save him. It's a good thing you got him here quickly."

With that, he disappeared through the doors and down the hall to the operating room. Lucy's knees started to buckle under her, but Jerry caught her. She sat back down and began to cry. All the tears she had kept in check flowed freely, and she couldn't stop.

Paul arrived with Vicki and went straight to Lucy. "Mom, what happened? Can you please tell me what happened out there? The two of you were going for a nice long ride. How did Cal end up with a bullet in him?"

He looked at her blood-streaked face where she had wiped the sweat off with her hands, which were also covered in blood.

"Mom?"

Lucy took a deep breath. "Caleb Kitson held a gun to my head. Cal shot him, and when he fell, his reflexes caused him to pull the trigger of his gun. That bullet found Cal."

That seemed like too simple of an explanation to Paul, but when he looked at Ben and his sisters, they all nodded to tell him it was enough for now.

Phoebe tried again, now that Lucy was fairly certain Cal would live. "Come on, Lucy. Let's get you cleaned up. The restroom is only a few feet away. You will be right here if the doctor comes back."

Lucy allowed her and Vicki to lead her to the restroom. She felt like she was walking through a fog and her feet each weighed a thousand pounds. Phoebe washed her face and hands. When they returned, Jackie handed her a cup of coffee. Lucy took it but her hands were shaking so much, it slopped over the edge of the cup, and she handed it back.

After several hours, the surgeon joined them once again. He spoke so they all could hear him, but directed his remarks to Lucy. "Your husband is in recovery right now. He will be moved to a room in ICU and from there, he will go to a regular room. It all depends on his oxygen levels. He's a healthy man in good physical shape, obviously, so his recovery should go well. I removed the bullet and the lobe where it was lodged. As I said before, he lost a major amount of blood, but if you hadn't packed it, he probably wouldn't have survived."

"Can I see him?" Lucy asked.

The doctor smiled at her. "For a bit, but not for too long. He has an incision that starts under his left breast area and continues around to his back. He's going to be mighty sore, but we have some meds for that."

He led the way to the recovery room. Lucy stepped in and went to the side of Cal's bed.

Thank you, God, for sparing his life. I will take good care of him, I promise.

She pulled the chair up to his bed. She put her head on the bed and cried. No one came to send her out of the room, so she stayed. After a very long time, she felt fingers threading through her hair. She raised her head. Cal had his hand on her head and one eye open.

Lucy told him, "Hey, Cowboy. I love you."

"Love you, too, Lucy," he said through dry lips and with a thick tongue. Then he closed his eyes again. The nurse came to check his vitals, but Lucy didn't leave.

Ben asked the nurse on duty if she knew what happened to the other man who was brought in with Cal. She told him she couldn't tell him that unless he was next of kin.

Ben wondered what would happen now. If Caleb died, would his dad be accused of murder? It was Lucy's word about what happened. There were no other witnesses. He wouldn't say anything about his concerns to the others. The immediate thing was to get Cal home and healthy again.

Jackie, Samantha, Paul, and Vicki all called their spouses to let them know Cal was out of surgery and in recovery. Ben had called Candy several times; he didn't want her to be too upset and go into labor prematurely. He did put into his memory bank what the doctor said about Lucy saving Cal's life.

Simon returned and was thanked by everyone for his part in the scenario and for his ability to fly a helicopter, which it seemed no one but Lucy knew about.

When Cal was moved to ICU several hours later, Lucy told the others to take a turn at seeing him, even though he wasn't fully aware of his surroundings yet.

Vicki gave her a bag with some clothes in it. "We wear about the same size, Mom, and I knew you weren't going to leave here to go home. There are several changes in there for you."

Lucy smiled at her "planning" daughter. "Thank you, Honey. You're right. I'm not leaving here without Cal."

Before Ben left, Lucy took him aside and asked, "Do you know where my gun is?"

"I have it, Lucy. I took it from you when you were threatening to make sure Caleb was no longer breathing."

Lucy vaguely remembered that, although the day's events were a bit of a blur after she found Cal sprawled on the ground.

"Thank you, Ben. I would hate to think Cal would recover and his wife would be in jail because she murdered someone. The last thing I remember clearly was Caleb unbuckling his belt and giving me the choice of a 'good time' with him, as he called it, or being shot in the head. I chose being shot, all the while hoping your father was somewhere where he could see what was happening and rescue me. He was, and he did...and in doing so, he saved my life."

"And from what the doctor said, you saved his."

"I know he's not even out of ICU yet, but I want to get him home where I can take care of him. Speaking of taking care of someone, you should go home and take care of Candy, Ben. I will be okay here with your dad, by myself."

* * *

Cal stayed in ICU for several days. It seemed he had tubes everywhere—one to drain his chest cavity, one for an IV to prevent infection, and one to help with oxygen levels. Slowly, over the course of several days, the doctor ordered them to be removed and for him to have breathing treatments. Cal would have to maintain an oxygen level of at least 90 before the doctor would release him. When he was moved to a normal hospital room, Lucy stayed in the room with him. He could not be released to go home for many more days. Visitors came to see him, but only Samantha and Jackie stayed for any length of time.

"Lucy, come lay by me?" Cal asked one evening after everyone had left and they were alone.

"Cal, your doctor will have a fit."

"I don't care. The tubes are gone, and I promise I won't move. I just want you next to me. Please?"

It was late at night, so Lucy climbed into his bed and lay next to him. "I was so afraid, Cal. I have never been that frightened in my entire life. I thought I was going to lose you, and I couldn't bear the thought of living life without you."

He held her hand, and they both fell asleep. When the night nurse made her rounds, she didn't have the heart to wake them. As she took his vitals, Cal opened his eyes and looked at her. He smiled and whispered, "Don't tell, okay? I needed her here by me."

The nurse nodded and promised not to tell if he didn't exert any energy.

When the doctor arrived the next morning, he shook his head. "I'm afraid to send you home if you are going to act like this," he laughed.

Lucy slid out of bed and tried to explain there had been no breaking of the rules.

The doctor became serious. "Cal, I'm going to release you. I have no doubt you will recover more quickly at home, but I have an entire list of restrictions. While I want you to build up your lungs and stamina, there are approved ways to do that. No driving, no lifting, no swimming, no mowing grass, no riding a horse, and no sexual activity. I will send a list of the restrictions home with you. There are things you need to do to build your body back to 'pre-trauma' stage. Lots of fluids; don't forget the fluids. You'll get there, I promise, but your body has taken a major hit, so don't screw it up, okay?"

He turned to Lucy and told her, "You need to ride herd on his activities, keep him on the straight and narrow…and don't tempt him too much." He winked at her and walked out of the room.

* * *

Before the discharge paperwork was completed, two detectives came to Cal's room. They wanted to speak to Cal and Lucy, individually. They needed their separate accounts of the shooting of Mr. Kitson, who, they said, had not survived his wounds.

"I hope you're not expecting me to shed any tears over that information," Lucy told them.

"No, Ma'am. We just need to hear, in your own words, what happened out there. If you don't mind, we'd like to speak to your husband alone, and then we'll ask you for your recollections."

Lucy left Cal's room and wandered to the nurses' station. She wanted to stay close so she would be available when the detectives were done questioning Cal.

Cal explained how he left Lucy sitting on the ground while he went to find her phone. Although he couldn't hear the words distinctly, he recognized Caleb's voice and from his hidden vantage point in the trees, he saw him point his gun at Lucy's head. That was when he shot him.

They asked more questions about the recent rustling and threats to the ranch. Cal answered as much as he knew. He suggested they contact the rangers for more information about the Kitson family and their operations.

Lucy was asked to come back into the room to give her version of the events of that day.

"I was removing a stone from my boot while Cal retraced our path to look for my phone. Caleb appeared and threatened to rape me or shoot me…or I suppose both, actually."

Cal had not heard that part. His face clouded over as he reached for Lucy's hand.

"I told him he would have to shoot me, because I wasn't going to willingly participate in his plans. He made the statement that either way, he would be getting even with my husband. He came within a few feet of me and pointed the gun directly at my head. That's when I heard the noise from Cal's revolver, and Caleb fell backward. As he was falling, his arm swung upward and his reflexes pulled the trigger. Of all the places that stray bullet could have gone, it found my husband."

The detectives wrote everything down. Then one of them asked, "Did you make any effort to save Mr. Kitson?"

Lucy shook her head. "I was too busy trying to keep Cal from bleeding to death. In fact, when my son-in-law wanted to load Mr. Kitson into the helicopter because he was still breathing, I offered to put him out of his misery. Ben, being a man of good moral character, stopped me and loaded him anyway."

"I believe we have everything we need. Thank you. I'm certain there will be no charges or grand jury investigations.

Your accounts concur, and the charges are consistent with everything we have on file about Caleb Kitson."

After they left the room, Cal pulled Lucy to him. "I didn't know everything he threatened to do, Lucy. I'm so sorry, but I'm not sorry he's no longer a threat to anyone."

* * *

Lucy used the phone at the nurses' station to call Phoebe. "Do you have a car yet?"

"Yes, we bought one last night, as a matter of fact. Why? Do you need a ride home?"

"Yes, the doctor released Cal, but it will be several hours before all the paperwork is ready. You can go to the ranch and get my car if you want to and bring it here. We'll drop you off at your house on our way home."

"Don't be silly. I'm looking for any excuse to drive my new one," she giggled. "Let me know in time to get there."

Chapter 24

LUCY WAS SHOWN how to change Cal's bandages and how to help him move from one place to another with the least amount of trauma to his incision. The respiratory therapist showed her the routine to increase his diminished lung function and sent pages of instructions.

Although he wasn't complaining, Lucy knew he was in a lot of pain while they were traveling. Ben came out to help get Cal inside the house and situated comfortably.

Lucy walked out with Phoebe to thank her before she left.

"Lucy, taking care of Cal will be a huge job for a while. I know you are aware of that, but I want you to know, Jerry and I will help in any way we can. We'll come and stay with him for a day or a few hours if you need a break, okay?"

"I appreciate it, and I'm sure I'll take you up on your offer. Taking care of John taught me a lot and gave me a much better perspective. At least Cal can walk and move around, although it is limited. He isn't restricted to bed like John was. The hardest part will be making sure he obeys the rules once he feels a little better."

Paul and Lynne stopped to see Cal before they went home. Jarrod looked like he might cry when he saw Cal. They had a special bond since they first met when Annie was in the hospital in Illinois.

"Can I sit by you," he asked, "or will that hurt?"

Cal patted the cushion next to him. "Come here, Jarrod. Right now, everything hurts, but it will get better. Your Grammy is going to take good care of me."

"Well, when we move here, I will come over and help Grammy take care of you, Grandpa Cal."

Lucy looked at Paul and Lynne, questioningly.

Paul smiled, "I guess Jarrod said it all, didn't he? If the offer is still good, we would very much like to rent the other ranch house, but we can discuss the details when Cal is feeling better."

Annie dejectedly sat down by Lucy. "They said I couldn't tell you until y'all talked, but now Jarrod did. He has a big mouth."

Lucy laughed as she hugged Annie. "She sounds like she's ready to move, with saying 'y'all' already. We are happy you'll be here. Now *y'all* have to tell me what colors of paint you would like."

"We have agreed to let you choose what you want, Lucy. We trust your judgment, but Annie would like her room to be pink again, if possible," Lynne said.

Lynne told Cal, "I want to hug you, but I'm not going to. I want you to know there were many prayers sent heavenward for you, and we're very happy you're home."

"I'm happy to be here, too. I'm happy to be alive, actually. I didn't think I was going to make it."

Candy and Ben came into the room from their house.

"We aren't staying, and I know Ben saw you when you got here, but I wanted to say welcome home," Candy told him.

Ben took Cal's hand and squeezed it. "I was scared, Dad." He was overcome with emotion and wiped a few tears that escaped. "I really was."

Cal nodded. "I know. I don't remember much, but I thank you for getting me in that helicopter."

"You should thank Lucy for knowing that Simon knew someone with a helicopter and that he knew how to fly one and had a license. I've known him a long time and didn't know that."

Cal smiled at Lucy. "She has a good memory, and we had a long time to talk when Simon flew us to Illinois."

Everyone wanted to hug Cal but squeezed his hands instead as they left for their own homes. Lucy brought his pain medication.

"Are you ready to get into some sweats so you're more comfortable?" She asked as she arranged pillows behind his back.

"In a minute, Lucy. I would actually be more comfortable if you would stop fussing for a bit and come sit by me. I'm not going to break if you touch me."

"I'm not worried about breaking you. I'm worried about hurting you or making your incision bleed. I can tell you, I saw enough blood a few days ago to last me a lifetime."

"On one of my doctor's early morning visits to my room, he said I should thank you for saving my life by slowing the loss of blood. How did you do that or what was he talking about?"

"I packed the wound with yarrow leaves like Grandpa taught me, but when he told me about it I never thought I'd have to actually *use* the information."

"It seems to me your grandfather and his wealth of information have saved my life two times now."

Lucy grew pensive. "He did teach me many factual things and a lot about life, too, I think. I didn't realize it when I was absorbing it all, but in retrospect, I can see it.

Cal drew her in and kissed her. "I can still kiss you; that isn't going to put me in danger."

"I don't know about that, Cowboy. It certainly could."

She stood up and told him, "Come on, let's get the breathing treatment done before I change the dressing and you get ready for bed."

* * *

The next few weeks were a progression of visits from friends and the kids and grandkids. Ben and Candy checked in every day with Ben giving Cal a daily "ranch report." Pastor Kelly and other friends from church visited.

John Lincoln, Cal's financial advisor, called and asked to come to the house with the forms and papers that needed to be signed. When he arrived, he apologized for the confusion on the day of their visit to his office. "He's young and definitely has a lot to learn in the area of people skills," John told them, describing the young man they spoke to initially. The forms were signed and dated and would be ready for their approval when Cal was feeling better.

Lucy had an idea she discussed with Cal. "When I checked on riding therapy schools, I found one located only five miles from Beaumont. If we check it out and think it would be beneficial for Gabe, we can offer to pay for it. Originally, I thought we could have him ride here, but I realized we don't have a clue about therapy riding."

Cal's instructions were to walk several times a day. At first, their walks were very short. Each day, they increased the distance by a few yards. Cal and Lucy walked together, down the drive and eventually, around the stables, even going as far as the bunkhouse where Lucy had to stand guard as the guys all wanted to greet him with a friendly slap on the back.

* * *

When Cal went back for a check-up several weeks later, the doctor was impressed with his progress.

"You are in extremely good physical shape, Cal, and that's about 90 percent of a patient's healing. I'll lift some of your restrictions, but not all of them. I don't want you driving yet or lifting more than 10 pounds. You can increase the number of stairs you climb, but if it causes you any difficulty in breathing, for heaven's sake, stop and rcst, okay?"

As they were leaving his office, he called Cal back in for a minute and shut the door.

"What was that all about?" Lucy asked as they left the office.

"He had a few more words of wisdom about some activities he forgot to mention. No horseback riding yet and no lawn work. I guess he doesn't realize I don't do lawn work even when I'm not restricted," he laughed.

* * *

Cal was becoming quite self-sufficient; he cleaned and organized the office, much to Ben's delight. He cleaned tack, brushed Cutter and the other riding horses, practiced every song he knew, and a few new ones, on his guitar, hung the pictures on the wall in the great room. and every other task Lucy could think of that didn't involve lifting or an excessive amount of upper body movement. She didn't want him to become too bored and frustrated. He climbed the stairs to the upstairs bedrooms every day as part of his recovery regimen. Most days, he was short of breath before he could make the trip up and down two times.

Lucy had time to concentrate on redecorating the other house. She chose the paint colors and hired a company to do the work. Another firm was removing the carpet and installing hardwood floors. She also had all the curtains and drapes taken down and replaced with new window treatments. August was quickly approaching, and she wanted everything to be ready for Paul and his family.

* * *

Cal went with Lucy when they visited the riding therapy school. They were both impressed with the dedication and knowledge of the instructors. Lucy invited Jackie and Gary and Gabe for dinner. She tried to remember Gabe's food preferences and prepared something he might eat. When Cal approached the subject of Gabe and his diagnosis, Jackie took Gary's hand and spoke quietly. "If this is about having an abortion, Dad, we've already made the decision not to do that. I don't believe I could have gone through with it, but I was so upset about ..." her voice trailed off. She still couldn't bring herself to say the word "autism."

"I'm very happy to hear that, Honey. You have no idea how happy...that's the best news you could possibly have given me. Lucy and I prayed you would reach that decision."

Cal continued, "I also want to talk to you about horseback riding for Gabe."

He gave them all the information he had, and Lucy shared many of the things Allen had told her along with a few places to find online support groups. She didn't want to totally overload them with information so she kept it simple. They agreed to try the riding for starters.

Before they left, Jackie sat next to Cal. "I was so afraid, Daddy, that you would be gone from my life forever. I couldn't even imagine that." She started to cry and put her head on his shoulder. "Holding Olivia at your birthday party and then almost losing you are the two things that made Gary and me realize how precious life really is and how much we need to treasure every minute of it, no matter how small that life might be." She ran her hand over her belly as if to reassure the baby inside that it would be loved and protected.

Cal put his arm around Jackie and hugged her. Perhaps his being shot was having some positive ripple effects, he thought.

Chapter 25

SAMANTHA, JACKIE, AND VICKI were still planning the baby shower for Candy and Ben. They chose the weekend after Lynne and Paul would be moved in so everyone could attend. They told Lucy she had had enough on her plate for the last six weeks so she could be a "guest" and enjoy the party. The boys certainly didn't care, but Amy, Annie, and Bethany were very excited at the prospect of attending a party for a new baby.

Vicki invited Lucy for lunch. They discussed what sort of things Ben and Candy needed. "Everything," Lucy laughed. "This is their first one, and there are no 'hand-me-downs' so they don't have much of anything. They do have the nursery painted and decorated, but it's almost completely empty."

"Mom, the reason I wanted to talk to you is to apologize, again, for being so upset with you after you spoke to Blake Tanner at the jail. We've been to the mediation hearing. I didn't tell you because you had enough to think about with taking care of Cal. Blake said he thought long and hard about what you told him. He only asked for one thing. He would like to have a picture each year on their birthdays. If he supplies his address, David and I don't have a problem with that. The mediator made it very clear to him before he signed the papers relinquishing his parental rights that this was a final thing. He would not be able to contact them or see them.

He understood and signed it. I almost felt sorry for him. It would be devastating to learn you had children and then almost immediately give them away. Maybe in the *far* future, Devon and Bethany will meet him but not until they are old enough to make that kind of decision."

"Will you still be afraid to take them somewhere or allow them to go somewhere without you or David close by?"

Vicki contemplated her answer. "Yes, I don't expect that feeling to go away any time soon. There are no guarantees for any parent that their child might not be abducted, but we will always trust God to protect them and keep them safe."

Lucy reached across the table and squeezed Vicki's hand. "I'm so thankful another nightmare seems to be over. Now if I can help Phoebe get her affairs in Illinois wrapped up, life might actually return to normal for a while."

When Lucy returned to the ranch, she found Cal on the front porch, waiting for her.

"Hi Honey. What's going on? You look like the Cheshire Cat with that *I have a secret* smile on your face."

He laughed at her and said, "I might have a secret. You never know. Actually, I have something to ask you; I need a *really* big favor."

"Okay," Lucy said hesitantly. "This isn't sounding good, Calvin Frasier. Just spit it out. What is it?"

Cal ran his fingers through his hair. "Actually, I've known about it for a few weeks, but I had Ben working on it. It seems we've hit an impasse, and now I need to ask you. Dolores, the camp cook, has to attend a family memorial of some sort, the third week in September. We have tried to find someone to replace her for that week, but aren't having any luck. Candy obviously can't do it, so I'm asking you. Alicia is Dolores' helper, and she would be there to help you, too, but she refuses to be in charge."

Lucy sat there looking at him as if he'd lost his mind. "Let me get this straight...you are asking the person who readily admits she isn't a cook to cook twice a day for how many men? Twenty?"

"Actually, it's closer to 30 this time of year, but what's 10 more, right?"

"No. I won't do it, Cal. Hire someone. Surely there's somebody who needs a job for a week. Put ads in the papers in Tomball and Montgomery."

"Ben and I have placed ads and looked. Really we have, but with no success. No one wants that kind of responsibility for only one week. Come on, Lucy. You like to say you can't cook, but that's not true. You're a good cook. It doesn't have to be anything fancy, just good tasting, filling food."

Ben had come home and was listening to their conversation before going inside.

"So, you're in on this, too, Ben?" Lucy asked.

"Dad and I agreed you were our only choice at this point, Lucy."

"What does this job pay, Mr. Frasier?" Lucy asked Cal.

He smiled and told her, "It has great benefits."

Lucy wagged her finger back and forth. "No. No, that won't get it. I already receive benefits. I'm talking real pay."

"Okay. How about this? You wanted to go along on the calf round-up in October, so you can go."

Lucy laughed at him, "Oh no. That won't fly either. I already won the right to go along when I won the bet about the gender of Vicki's baby. Did you forget that?"

"Apparently. Okay, what do you want?" Cal hesitated for a bit before adding, "I know I'm going to be sorry I asked that."

Ben was laughing but not saying anything. He already knew who had the best negotiating skills.

Lucy looked at Cal for a while, without saying a word. Finally, she told him. "I want a cutting horse, a good one. Not a tired, worn-out one from the rodeo circuit. I want good breeding, and I want it trained well."

"So, you're telling me if you cook for one week, it's going to cost me roughly $20,000?"

"You got it, Cowboy," Lucy said. "Take it or leave it, but it seems to me you're kind of over a barrel here. Oh and by the way, I still expect benefits."

She turned and went into the house.

"Nice negotiating," Ben told him while laughing.

"Don't tell Lucy, but I would have bought her any horse she wanted, even if she didn't agree to cook for a week."

Ben nodded, "I know you would've, Dad, and I won't tell her but I think she already knows that."

Cal went inside. "So…you think you outsmarted me, huh?"

"Nope, not at all. But I do recognize a desperate man when I see one," she laughed as she put her arms around him.

"I *am* a desperate man, Lucy." He unbuttoned the top buttons on her shirt.

"No, no, no, Cal. We have been so good for many weeks. We have followed the doctor's orders. We can't mess it up now. He has to approve your 'activities' remember?"

"He already has. The last time I was there, he told me when I could walk up and down the long stairway to the upstairs bedrooms three times in a row without having to stop and catch my breath, I was *good to go,* as he put it. I have been going up and down for weeks and for the last three days, I have not had to stop, not even for a few seconds." He finished unbuttoning her shirt and pulled her to him. Their kiss lasted longer than their conversation had.

* * *

Lucy lay with her head cradled in the bend of Cal's arm. "I think *I'm* having trouble breathing," Lucy laughed. Then she asked, "You know I would have cooked for the men without pay, right?"

"Yes, and I would have bought you anything you wanted, Lucy, even if you said no to the cooking. You know that, too, right?"

"Yes. That's what love looks like, isn't it?" She traced her finger along the incision scar on his chest. "I can't even begin to tell you how many emotions I experienced that day in the woods and later, in the hospital. Do you realize we haven't known each other a year and we have experienced more trauma and drama than most people do in a lifetime? I never gave up hope you would survive, Cal. I could not believe God would take you from me after finally letting me know what true happiness feels like."

Cal touched the scar on her cheek that was still faintly visible. "We all have scars, don't we? Maybe scars are God's way of reminding us how much we need him in our lives, so we never forget and stop thanking him for his protection and his sacrifice for us."

* * *

Ben told Candy, "Well, Dad just spent $20,000 for a cook for a week."

Candy's eyes opened wide. "What? How did he do that? Does Lucy know?"

"Oh, she knows. That's who he spent it on," Ben laughed.

Candy said, "I'm going over there and find out what you're talking about, Ben."

Ben grabbed her arm, gently, and told her, "I don't think I'd go over there right now, Honey. I think they might be discussing the terms of the agreement." Then he smiled at her and kissed her.

* * *

Cal and Lucy decided to buy the furniture for the nursery as their gift to Ben and Candy, but they let them choose the kind they wanted. It was delivered and set up in the nursery; the only thing missing was a baby.

When the moving truck arrived from Oklahoma, Ben, Gary, David, and Sean all came to help place the furniture where Lynne wanted it. Lucy would not allow Cal to lift anything yet even though he thought he could. Annie was ecstatic about her pink room, and Jerrod kept wandering from room to room, saying, "I'm going to have a real horse, I'm going to have a real horse."

The invitations had been sent for the shower. The girls invited Candy's friends from church, her closest friend who was pregnant at Ben and Candy's wedding, Phoebe, and against Candy's better judgment, they sent one to her mother. Candy was sure she wouldn't come, but she said they could send it.

Several days later, there was a knock on the door after breakfast. Lucy answered and found Candy standing there with a piece of mail in her hand. "I knew this would happen," she said with tears in her eyes. "I just knew it."

"Come in, Candy and tell me what's going on," Lucy said as she pulled her inside and closed the door.

"My mom, who couldn't even find time to come to my wedding, is now going to come for the shower and possibly, stay until the baby comes."

"Oh, Candy, I know this is upsetting to you, but it might be nice for her to be here."

"No, it won't, Lucy. She always spoils everything by trying to take over and make all the decisions, even if it's something she knows nothing about. I'm not coming to my own shower."

Lucy hugged her. "Yes, you are, Candy. You're the guest of honor. It will be okay. Your four sisters-in-law are strong women. They will handle your mother. When is she coming, and do you think she would prefer to stay in the guest house or the rooms upstairs?"

Candy handed Lucy the note in her hand. Lucy read it, and then looked at Candy. "Oh, I can see why you're upset. She's planning on coming for the shower and staying until the baby's born? That could be a month if your due date is correct."

"I knoooow," Candy cried. "She can't be here that long. I'll run away from home."

Lucy put her arms around Candy. "It's okay, Honey. We'll think of something. Maybe after she's here for a bit, we can dissuade her from staying that long. You know, she might be really bored out here in 'no man's land.' We'll take it one day at a time. First, we'll pick her up from the airport and get her settled in the guest house. Then we'll see how it goes. Ben will not allow anyone or anything to upset you, Candy."

Candy smiled and blew her nose. "You're right. Ben will take care of everything. What are the guys doing during the shower? Usually, they're invited, too, aren't they?"

"Yes, but I think the girls thought the little boys would be better off going to see a movie with the big boys. I'm not sure about Gabe, though. He won't like the movie; there will be too much stimulation for him. The shower won't be a good place for him, either. Maybe Cal can take him somewhere. Gabe would go just about anywhere with Cal, I think."

CHAPTER 26

BEN AND CANDY drove to the airport to pick up Candy's mother when she arrived on Friday, the day before the shower.

"Hi Mom. You've never met my husband, Ben. Ben, this is my mother, Myrna."

"Hello, Ben. Please be careful with that red bag. It's new, and I don't want it scuffed or scratched. It's really hot here...I hope your car has air conditioning. How far is it to this house you live in? You certainly are big, Candy. Are you sure you aren't having twins or triplets?"

"Mom. Stop with the questions, okay? Yes, it's hot; this is August, in Texas. Of course, our car has AC, you won't find many here that don't, and it is at least a 45-minute drive home, depending on traffic, and I'm having just one baby, okay?"

Ben smiled to himself. He didn't think Candy was going to need his help fending off her mother. It seemed to him, she was pretty good at it.

Lucy was waiting for them when they arrived. She stepped out onto the porch to greet Candy's mother.

"Hello, Myrna," she said as she extended her hand. "I trust you had a good flight?"

Myrna shook Lucy's hand and commented, "It was all right. Seemed like forever."

"Yes, I'm certain it did. But you're here now, and that's the main thing. Let's get you settled in the guest house. I'm sure you'll find it has everything you need. If not, give me a call, and I will find whatever it is you're missing."

"There's a guest house?" Myrna asked incredulously as she looked at the imposing outside of the ranch house.

"Yes and you get it all to yourself." Lucy laughed. "Why don't you come in and have a glass of lemonade while Ben takes your bags? We need to get Candy inside, too."

Lucy poured ice-cold lemonade into tall glasses for everyone. She had Candy set in the chair with a foot stool in front of it. "Put your feet up, Sweetie. You've been riding and standing for too long."

Myrna surveyed the great room. "So, you all live here together?" she asked.

"Sort of," Lucy explained. "Ben and Candy have the house on that end, and Cal and I have the house on this end. This room that connects them is a multi-purpose room or as we call it, the great room. The girls will be here later to decorate it for the shower tomorrow."

Myrna seemed aloof and not at all interested in her daughter, but when Cal came in from outside and was introduced to her, she immediately started a conversation with him. *So that's how it's going to be,* Lucy chuckled to herself. *Save your breath, Myrna.*

Jackie, Vicki, and Lynne arrived to decorate the great room. Samantha was coming later because she and Amy were going to stay overnight. They suggested Candy show her mother the nursery, but once Cal left the room, Myrna was more interested in telling them how to decorate.

Lucy could see Candy's frustration level rising. She took Myrna by the arm and guided her outside. "Why don't we see if Ben got everything put in the guest house for you? I'll help you put your things away, if you want."

"Did Candy's father tell her he's coming for the birth, too?" Myrna asked.

Lucy paused for a second. "No, I don't believe so. I think Candy would have told me if he had. Do you know when he's planning on getting here?"

"Not exactly. We rarely speak to each other, but I did let him know I was coming today, so he will probably show up soon. He never wants to be outdone by me. Do you have another guesthouse?"

"No, but we have bedrooms above the great room. He can stay there."

Lucy contemplated whether or not to tell Candy, afraid it would turn into her worst nightmare.

Cal commented on the food Lucy served for dinner. "You outdid yourself, Honey. What's up with all the delicious food?"

She smiled sweetly at him and muttered, "I'm practicing for my new job."

* * *

The day of the shower, the men and boys left for a movie, while Cal and Gabe went into town for an ice cream treat and then to the park.

The shower was a success, with the little girls enjoying every minute of it and Olivia Rose sleeping through the entire thing. Candy was delighted with each gift she opened; they ranged from the practical to the whimsical. Due to the fact no one knew the gender of the baby, there were no definite "boy" or "girl" clothes.

Myrna complained, "If you had found out, it would've been a lot easier to purchase something, Candy."

"I know, but Ben and I wanted to wait until the baby was born. It will be a surprise for us, too."

Myrna frowned, indicating she thought that was the dumbest thing she ever heard of.

After the "boys" returned and ate, everyone left, including Myrna, who declared she needed a nap.

Candy enjoyed showing all the gifts to Ben, even though she looked as though she was the one who needed a nap. Lucy offered to help her put everything away tomorrow. One of the gifts was a stroller, so the receiving blankets and smaller things were placed into the stroller, while the rest could remain in stacks in the great room for the time being.

"How was your afternoon with Gabe?" Lucy asked when they were alone.

Cal chuckled. "It was great. Now that a speech therapist has been working with him and teaching him some simple sign language, he is quite the 'talker.' I think I'm going to have to take a class, so I know what he's saying. Gary told me the therapist believes he will say words eventually, but for now, at least he has a way to communicate a little bit."

"I invited Myrna to attend church with us tomorrow, but she declined. I bet she would go if you asked her," Lucy poked him in the ribs and laughed.

Cal frowned, "Yeah, what was up with her talking my ear off when we were introduced?"

"Face it, Cowboy; you're irresistible to all women and especially so when your shirt was sticking to your sweaty body."

"Really?" he laughed at her. He kissed her and said, "I'm only interested in being irresistible to one woman."

Cal and Lucy went to church by themselves. Ben stayed home with Candy, who was exhausted and complaining of a backache.

* * *

Ben came over on Monday morning. "Candy's so upset. Her father called; he's going to show up early, too. I guess he has to be here if her mother is here. I suggest we put them in the guest house together and maybe they can work out their differences. Her due date isn't for two weeks yet. What's the matter with these people? Obviously, they don't care about how Candy feels or what all this stress is doing to her."

"When is he coming?' Lucy asked, thinking of the sheets that needed to be changed and the upstairs bathroom that would need to be cleaned before he got there.

"I'm going to pick him up this afternoon. Maybe I can talk to him. I hope he's more reasonable than her mother seems to be."

* * *

Lucy decided she definitely liked Frank better than Myrna. He seemed pleasant, grateful for the place to stay, and considerate of Candy's feelings. But he and Myrna together were like oil and water. They were going to have to *suck it up* and get along or this was going to be a long two weeks.

Cal told Lucy, "On Wednesday Ben and I are taking the stock trailer to pick up the new bull we bought. Ben's concerned about Candy, but we'll only be gone for a few hours. I don't feel comfortable going by myself yet, in case we need extra muscle to load the animal. Do you think it will be all right?"

"I think so. I'll be here if she needs to go to the hospital suddenly, and Frank and Myrna are here, although any help from them is questionable."

As Cal and Ben were preparing to leave on Wednesday morning, Lucy told Ben. "Do not let your dad do anything he shouldn't do yet. I don't care if it means leaving the danged bull there, okay?"

Ben nodded. "I promise I will take good care of him, Lucy."

She checked on Candy several times during the day, knowing the guys should be home soon.

Cal called to say they had run into some difficulties and would be home later than expected.

"How much later? Do you have any idea?" Lucy questioned.

"It shouldn't be more than a few hours. The man we were meeting was delayed in getting here so now we are behind schedule. Ben wanted me to ask if Candy is okay and if her back feels any better."

"She was resting when I checked on her a little bit ago but still complaining about her back. That kind of pain is pretty normal when you're in the last stages of pregnancy."

As Lucy was preparing a sandwich for herself, Candy opened the door and just stood there.

"What's wrong, Honey?" Lucy asked and then noticed a puddle of water at Candy's feet.

"Oh my goodness, Candy. Obviously, your water has broken. Have you been having contractions?"

Candy shook her head. "I don't know. I guess I have been having them, off and on, since yesterday, maybe, but I didn't know what they were. I thought it was just a backache all day. I didn't realize it was coming and going."

Lucy dried her hands. "Okay. Let's think about this. If you've been having contractions for over a day, this birth could be imminent. We'll call your doctor, and I'll drive you to the hospital in Tomball, okay? And we'll call Ben; he can meet us there."

Candy held her belly and cried out as another pain took over. Frank came down the stairs to see what was going on. Lucy told him to time the contractions if he had a watch. She then called Candy's doctor and surprisingly, reached him. She explained the situation and told him Candy had been having contractions for over 24 hours, they were less than two minutes apart, and her water had broken.

"You'll never get her to Tomball in time if they're that close together. I'll call the hospital and have them send the ambulance for her. In the meantime, have her lay down. A paramedic will call and give you instructions. I think you better get ready to deliver a baby."

Lucy didn't want to panic Candy, although she was panicked enough for both of them. "Listen, Sweetie, we're going to have you lie down, okay?" She told Frank to get the air mattress that was still blown up and standing in the corner of the great room where the kids played with it after the shower. She put a couple of blankets on it and helped Candy lie down.

Lucy nervously waited for the phone call from the paramedics. It seemed like an hour before the phone rang, although it was only a matter of minutes.

"Yes?" Lucy answered.

"Hi. This is Carly. The EMTs are on their way but until they get there, I'm going to walk you through this birth, okay? Don't be nervous. I've done this many times. Can I have your name, please?"

"It's Lucy."

"Hello Lucy. Can I ask if you have had children?"

"Yes, I've had two, but I wasn't on this end of the action," Lucy said as she pulled her hair back and fastened it into a ponytail.

Carly laughed. "I understand. Place the phone close to you and put it on speaker so your hands are free. Can you hear me loud and clear?"

"Yes."

"Okay. I need you to have the patient lie down."

"She already is. On an air mattress, covered with blankets."

"Good. Now remove her clothes from the waist down. Cut them off if you have to. I'll wait."

"Frank, grab the scissors on the desk and for heaven's sake, call Ben and tell him he needs to get here, somehow."

"I hope this isn't your favorite pair of shorts and underwear, Candy," Lucy quipped as she cut through both and removed them.

Carly continued, "Now that you have removed her clothing, raise her head with pillows, if you can, and have her pull her knees up and apart, but do not let her sit up."

Myrna came in the door and looked horrified at what she saw. Frank grabbed two pillows off the couch and placed them under Candy's head. Then he sat by her and let her squeeze his hand until it nearly turned purple. Candy was having more contractions, and Myrna looked as if she would faint.

"Now, I want you to get some dry towels and a blanket to wrap the baby in. Also, get a string or a shoelace; anything to tie off the cord later. Is the mother pushing yet?"

"Yes, she is, but not extremely hard."

"Okay. It's good for her to not push too hard at this point."

Carly continued, "Now, look closely at her vagina and tell me how close the baby is to being born. Can you see any part of the baby yet?"

"No, not yet."

"Okay, you have a bit of time. Reassure the mother that help is on the way and let me know if anything changes."

"Candy, Ben is on his way home and the paramedics are on their way. Keep that in mind, okay, Sweetie? You're doing great."

"I can't do this," Candy said between contractions.

"Yes, you can. You're a strong young woman and the end result will be worth the pain. We'll do it together. You're surrounded by people who love you, so let's get this done."

Candy squeezed her father's hand and pushed through another contraction.

"Can you see any part of the baby now," Carly asked again.

"Yes, the very top of the head," Lucy replied.

Frank stood up and took Myrna's arm. Quietly, he told her, "Either set down and support Candy or go outside . . . now. She doesn't need you pacing and whining. Understand?"

She nodded and sat on the floor by Candy's head. "It will be all right," she told her as she wiped the perspiration off Candy's face.

"Okay," Carly said. "With each contraction, I want you to place your palm against her vagina and apply gentle but firm pressure to keep the baby's head from delivering too fast and tearing her. Do you understand?"

"Yes, I understand, and I'm doing that now. The doctor said this is a big baby, Carly."

"That's okay. You're doing great. When the contractions get closer and harder, be prepared to grab the baby. Remember to support the baby as it comes out. It will be very slippery. Don't drop it."

Lucy couldn't help but laugh out loud at that instruction. She would try her best not to drop the baby.

Candy screamed and gave one last push. The baby was in Lucy's hands.

"Is the baby completely out now?" Carly asked.

"Yes, I'm holding him," Lucy said. "It's a boy."

"Is he breathing, and is that a healthy cry I hear?"

"Yes, he's crying," Lucy told her. "Screaming, actually," she added.

"Good. Now wipe off the baby's mouth and nose and wrap him in a clean, dry towel or blanket. Cover his head."

"Myrna, hand me one of those little hats off the stack of gifts, and some more receiving blankets."

Lucy wiped the baby's face and nose, removing the slippery white substance. She placed her finger in his mouth to remove any mucus lodged in there. Myrna put the hat on the baby's head, and Lucy placed him in the blankets.

"Without pulling the cord tight, put the baby on the mother's belly or in her arms, making sure the cord is not wrapped around the baby's neck," Carly continued.

"Now listen carefully. Take the string you have and tie it tightly around the umbilical cord…6 inches from the baby. Do *not* cut the cord."

Frank helped as Lucy's fingers were wet and slippery and it was difficult to tie the string.

"Okay, it's done," Lucy told her.

"Do not pull on the cord. The placenta will deliver soon. When it does, wrap it in a towel; the doctor will want to check it. Is it out yet?"

"No, not yet."

"It will be soon. In the meantime, keep the mother warm and check the baby's breathing often. Tell me when the EMTs arrive."

At that precise moment, the EMTs came in the door, followed closely by Ben and Cal.

Ben went immediately to Candy and the baby. Tears were coursing down his cheeks. "I'm so sorry, Candy. I'm so sorry I wasn't here."

"It's okay, Ben. Look at our beautiful son. He's perfect…and I love you."

The EMTs checked the baby and Candy. "You did a good job…all of you," the EMT told them as they put Candy and the baby into the ambulance. Ben joined them, still crying and smiling at the same time.

When they were all gone, Lucy looked at Cal and started to cry, too, now that the whole thing was over. He sat down on the floor next to her and put his arms around her.

"Sweetheart, I can't ever leave you alone, can I? You seem to find some new adventure every time I do," Cal told her as he pushed the escaped strands of wet hair off her face and tucked them behind her ears.

"Mmmm, yes, this was an adventure, all right." She looked at her wet and bloody clothes. "No wonder doctors wear gowns," she said.

Frank and Myrna were standing outside on the deck with their arms around each other's waists. "Well, that's a first," Lucy observed, nodding toward them.

"Come on, I'll help you clean up this mess, and then I have a surprise for you."

"I really can't handle any more surprises today, Cal."

"Just one more, okay?"

When things were mostly cleaned up, including Lucy, Cal led her outside where Ben had hurriedly parked the truck and trailer.

He helped her get into the truck without looking in the trailer and drove it to the stables.

"You're going to put that bull in the stable with the horses?" Lucy questioned, raising her eyebrows to indicate she didn't approve of that idea.

Cal opened the back of the trailer, climbed inside and backed a horse out.

"Here's your cutting horse, Cowgirl. His name is Rigbee. I expect nothing but the best meals for the crew in exchange for this big guy," he laughed. "Do you think you can handle him?"

For the second time in an hour, Lucy was crying. "Cal, he's beautiful. You were never going to get a bull?"

"We have purchased one, but we'll have to go back for him. I wanted to give you this today. That's why we were later than expected. He wasn't at the appointed meeting place."

"I'm sure I can handle him with a little practice. You just wait and see, Cowboy."

Chapter 27

CAL AND LUCY drove to the hospital to take Ben's car to him and to see the new baby now that he would be cleaned up. They quietly entered Candy's room. The baby was in a bassinet, sleeping. When Ben saw them, he hugged Lucy so tightly, that he picked her up off the floor.

She suppressed a giggle, trying not to wake the baby. "Well, I'm happy to see you, too, Ben," she whispered.

"I don't know how we can ever thank you, Lucy."

"Candy did all the hard work. I just prayed a lot and caught that baby boy," she told him.

Cal hugged Candy and then gave Ben a hug. "Congratulations, Son. It's an indescribable feeling when you see your newborn child. I remember how I felt when you and the girls were born."

Lucy was caressing the baby's cheek. "He is beautiful. Have you chosen a name?"

Ben took Candy's hand. "We have. It's Luke Calvin Frasier. Luke was as close as we could get to your name, Lucy, and we wanted him to have both of your names."

"What an incredible honor. Thank you," Lucy told them.

* * *

"Are you okay, Sweetheart?" Cal asked when they were on their way home. "Did helping Luke into the world make you sad for some reason?"

"No, not sad…maybe pensive is the word. I remember thinking when my children were born, I had forever to spend time with them and teach them, but in an incredibly short amount of time…they grew up. I want to tell Ben and Candy not to spend time worrying about doing everything right and just love him to pieces."

Frank was going to leave a bit sooner than anticipated originally. Now that the baby was here, he was anxious to get back home. Myrna also changed her flight plans, although she stayed for a few days after Frank left. They both spent as much time with Candy and Luke as they could, obviously enjoying being grandparents again.

Myrna asked Lucy if she could join her on her morning walk each day.

On one of those walks, Myrna said, "I'm sure you've wondered why Candy and I don't have a good relationship, why I don't act like a mother to her."

"It's none of my business, Myrna. I do know Candy feels you don't care about her, but perhaps that will change now that you both have Luke to love."

Myrna was silent for a long time, but finally said, quietly, "Candy's not my daughter."

Lucy nearly tripped over her own feet. She stopped walking and touched Myrna's arm. "What did you say?"

"Candy is Frank's daughter, but not mine. He had an affair; the girl became pregnant and died during childbirth. Frank confessed everything to me, asked for my forgiveness and pleaded with me to take the baby into our family. I thought I could do it, but every time I looked at Candy and her red hair, I was reminded of Frank's unfaithfulness. He probably did 80 percent of the day-to-day taking care of her. I know he was never unfaithful again, but my attitude eventually destroyed our marriage."

Lucy asked, "And Candy has no clue about this? Didn't your boys wonder where a baby came from? I mean, especially the older ones?"

Myrna shrugged, "They were still pretty young, and kids didn't know everything about babies and sex then, like they do today. I'm sure now that they are adults, they have figured it out, mainly because of her red hair, but we never discuss it. Unfortunately, they aren't close to Candy either, probably because of my actions toward her."

Lucy saw tears roll down Myrna's cheeks as she said, "I seem to have messed up a whole lot of lives due to my inability to forgive. Please don't tell anyone I shared this with you. I don't know why I did; I have never admitted it to a soul.

"I won't tell anyone but Cal. I don't keep any secrets from him, but you don't have to worry about him saying anything." Lucy continued, "Do you and Frank still have feelings for each other? Neither one of you remarried, and I saw you after Luke was born; it seemed to draw you together. You know, it's never too late to forgive and make things right, even if you don't have any intention of getting back together."

"I suppose you're right, although the person I would really like to apologize to is Candy. Seeing her with Luke makes me realize how cold and unloving I have been to her for her entire life, but I can't do that without telling her the truth, and now is not the time for that."

"Do you pray, Myrna? Or perhaps I should ask if you have a relationship with Jesus?"

"No, not really. That went out the window with Frank's betrayal, too, and I've never looked for it again. That's probably the reason I'm such a negative, hateful old woman."

"It really is our choice as to what our attitude is going to be. We can choose each day if we're going to be happy or hateful. That doesn't mean everything goes according to our plans, but it does mean God grants us the strength and courage to deal with the obstacles," Lucy told her.

She continued, "Myrna, just so you know…I'm going to pray this entire mess gets straightened out somehow. Your family, and especially you and Frank, and Candy, of course, deserve a life where you do not have to carry this secret with you any longer."

"Thank you, Lucy, for the prayers and for listening and not judging."

Lucy saw Frank and Myrna conversing and occasionally walking together, in the days before they each went their separate ways again. Perhaps the secrets could be eliminated, even if their relationship couldn't be repaired.

* * *

As Lucy was pulling her night shirt over her head, she said, "Cal, I'm going to talk to Dolores one morning and take notes on all the things I should know before I take her place for a week. Do you know what time she starts in the morning?"

Cal hesitated, but then said, "I believe she gets things started around 4 o'clock."

Lucy was crawling into bed when he said that. "Four o'clock? In the morning? As in, before it's daylight? You have got to be kidding me, Calvin Frasier. You didn't mention anything about 4 a.m. when we struck this deal."

"Maybe not," Cal laughed. "But you already have your payment; there's no backing out now."

Lucy got as close to him as possible and told him, "I believe there was some mention of benefits, too, Cowboy. Just so you know…those benefits had better be retroactive because if I have to be at the bunkhouse at the ungodly hour of 4 o'clock, I will be in bed each night by 7 and probably too tired to collect any benefits, anyway. Okay?"

"Okay, Baby. We'll make them retroactive until we go to Chicago to celebrate your birthday in November. It was going to be a surprise, but I have to redeem myself a little bit, so I'll tell you about it. Phoebe and Jerry and you and I are going to the Windy City to celebrate. I hope you still have your winter coat and boots somewhere."

"I do, but why are you taking me back there? I thought you never wanted to see that city again."

Cal reached for her and pulled her into his arms. "I remember when we first met and I asked why you stayed in Illinois. You said you liked the lights and excitement and downtown, especially at Christmastime, so I wanted to give that to you. We're going to stay on The Magnificent Mile; you and Phoebe can *shop 'til you drop,* and Jerry and I will pay the bills and carry the bags, okay?"

"I don't know what to say. The fact you remembered what I liked is more amazing to me than any shopping I might do." She ran her hands over his shoulders and down his bare chest. "Cal, I love you to pieces, and since I'm not going anywhere at 4 *tomorrow* morning, what do you say we get an early start on those benefits?"

* * *

"Good morning, Dolores," Lucy said a few mornings later, as she walked through the door of the kitchen, situated on the far end of the bunkhouse. "I don't know what Mr. Frasier pays you, but I'm definitely going to tell him you need a raise to be here every morning at this ridiculous hour."

Dolores laughed, causing her ample body to shake all over. "You don't have to do that, Miz' Frasier. Mr. Frasier always pays well."

"Yes, he does, Dolores," Lucy chuckled. "Please call me Lucy. That goes for you, too, Alicia," she told the young woman who entered the kitchen, her arms laden with ingredients for making breakfast.

"Tell me again; how many do you prepare for?"

"It changes with the time of year, but right now, it's usually 30 men for breakfast, and then we pack everything they'll need for lunch in the field," Dolores told her. "Mr. Frasier likes things done the traditional way. He says the only thing missing is the chuck wagon pulled by mules." She gave Lucy the menus she used and showed her where everything was located—the pots, pans, skillets, utensils, and all the staple food items.

"You can prepare anything you want, Miz' Frasier…Lucy. It doesn't have to be fancy; just 'stick to your ribs' kind of cooking."

"That's the kind I do best, Dolores," Lucy assured her. "I'm not so good with the fancy stuff. I promise I'll make certain your cowboys don't leave here hungry." She continued to reassure Dolores. "I actually spent several weeks cooking in the kitchen of an inner-city mission when I was in college. A group of students from my business class were supposed to learn how the finances were done for a non-profit, but somehow I ended up in the kitchen. I think my grandmother had something to do with that, since she was sure I would be an old maid if I didn't learn to cook."

She watched Alicia mix pancake batter. Then, to practice for next week, Lucy poured it on a griddle half as big as her kitchen table. As she was flipping them, she smiled thinking how long it would take Cal to make monkey pancakes with this much batter.

* * *

During dinner that evening, Cal asked, "How did your training session go this morning?"

"It was good. Dolores is a sweet person who I think is concerned that I won't feed her 'boys' enough, but she doesn't have a choice, so she's willing to give it a shot. Alicia is as cute as a button, a very hard worker, and I think some young guy named Toby is sweet on her. We'll get it done, Cal, and I promise no one will starve."

"I overheard some of the guys talking today. They're a bit worried, too, but not about your cooking. They're worried about remembering to mind their manners around the boss's wife."

"Maybe they should be," Lucy laughed. "A couple of them are definitely surly in the morning."

"I'll go with you at 4 on Monday morning," Cal offered.

"No, Honey," Lucy said emphatically, shaking her head. "You can come and eat when the rest of the guys do, but I don't want you there when we're preparing the food. You'll make me nervous."

"Nervous? Is this the same woman who used to face down the bad guys and carries a gun with her? You're going to be nervous?"

Lucy smiled at him. "This is totally different. I think I'd rather be facing down the bad guys."

* * *

Monday was going like clockwork until she went to the stove to take a pan of biscuits out of the oven and someone stole up behind her and put his arms around her waist in a bear hug. Without turning to see who it was, she said, "If I drop these biscuits on the floor, I'm going to beat you with the empty pan."

A flustered young cowhand dropped his hands and tried explaining. "I'm so sorry. Oh my gosh, I am so sorry. I thought you were Alicia. I'm truly sorry."

Alicia walked up to him with eyes the size of saucers. "Toby, what do you think you're doing? In the first place, you shouldn't be in here when I'm working, and do you know that's Mrs. Frasier?"

Cal saved him by saying, "Listen, Toby, you squeeze your girl, okay? But I'll take care of squeezing mine." Every man in the room was laughing as Toby's cheeks turned a bright red.

* * *

The days passed with no other incidents. There was one cowhand named Len who complained every day about the fact that Lucy was going along on the round-up. He never said it to her face but always loud enough for her to hear.

On Friday, she had had enough. She confronted him at the table where he was seated and asked, "What is it that bothers you so much about my going along?"

"The round-up ain't no place for a woman. They get in the way, they complain about being hot and dusty, and it slows everything down. This kitchen is a good place for you but not on a horse when we're trying to work cattle."

It suddenly became so quiet in the room, all you could hear was the nervous scuffling of some boots on the wooden floor. Cal came into the back of the room just in time to hear what was said but was only going to step in if Lucy couldn't handle Len, and he was sure she could.

"Really? Is that really what you think, or are you purposely trying to tick me off?" Lucy didn't wait for an answer. "I can understand how you might feel that way, but

I can assure you I will not be a liability. I can ride, shoot, and rope as well as any man here, including you, Len."

He laughed at her. "That'll be the day. You're only allowed to go because you're the boss's wife."

Cal stepped up before Lucy could knock Len off the bench and told him, "I have a great idea, Len. We'll have a contest. Everyone gets to compete, including Lucy. I already know what she can do, but let's show everyone else, okay? We'll set it up for two weeks from Saturday, in the corral. Is that good enough for you, Len?"

Len grunted and nodded. Before he went out the door, Cal spoke to him one more time. "Oh, and Len, a word of advice: you better bring your 'A' game."

* * *

Cal and Lucy sat on the front porch in the evening. Lucy sat with her back to him as he massaged her shoulders. "That feels so good. Every muscle is sore, I think. On the plus side…the week's over, no one got food poisoning, and I didn't hear any complaints…about the food, at least. It was a good experience but if Dolores ever quits, I don't want the job permanently."

Ben and Candy brought Luke out and joined them. "I hear you have a challenge, Lucy," Ben teased. "Two weeks from Saturday, is it?"

Lucy rolled her eyes. "Ask your dad. He's the one who set it up. I was holding my own with Len."

Cal nodded, "Yes, you were, but I saw the fire come into your eyes when he said you belonged in the kitchen. I was trying to protect my hired hand."

"I realize Rigbee is a very well trained animal, but for us to work well together, we have to become so attuned to each other, we move like one. I don't know if two weeks is long enough, Cal."

"You've already been working him; you'll both do fine. This isn't the championships at the Houston Rodeo, you know."

"Maybe. I guess we'll see, won't we? One more thing I've been meaning to ask you. Where did the phrase, "Bring your 'A' game" come from? I've heard it many times, but I've never heard *you* say it. You surprised me."

Cal shrugged his shoulders, "I don't know. It seemed appropriate for the situation. Len better bring his best game, if he doesn't want to be humiliated."

* * *

Candy placed Luke in Lucy's arms. Lucy smoothed Luke's wispy red hair and coaxed a smile from him.

"Mom called just to chat a little and ask how the baby was doing. She has never called me. I don't know what changed."

"Babies have a way of changing lives, Candy. Maybe being a part of the birth gave her a new perspective..." she glanced at Cal "...on lots of things."

* * *

When they were back inside, Cal reminded Lucy she didn't have to go to bed while it was still light outside because she didn't have to get up and be at work at 4 the next morning.

"That's right, I don't. I almost forgot I can sleep in, if I want to. And...we can go back to having our prayer time in the morning instead of at night. I think there were several nights I fell asleep in the middle of our prayers."

Lucy walked to the living room. "So, tell me, since I don't have to go to bed so early, do you have plans for this evening, Cowboy?"

"I think I might have," Cal told her.

"Okay, well...make sure you bring your 'A' game," she laughed.

Chapter 28

LUCY SPENT AS MUCH TIME on Rigbee as she could. She was nowhere near being a rider of professional or even amateur skill level, but she had spent a lot of hours working cattle when she was a kid and young adult. She knew how to separate a cow from the herd and let her horse do the rest. Rigbee was a responsive horse, and if she didn't outperform Len, she would at least give him a run for his money. She was confident in her ability to rope a calf and handle a pistol, but her rifle skills weren't as good as she'd like them to be.

When Saturday morning arrived, Cal found her dressed and ready to go. She was wearing jeans, boots, chaps, long-sleeved shirt, bandana, gloves, and cowboy hat. "You will definitely be the best-looking contestant this morning," Cal told her.

"I'll take that as a compliment, since I'll also be the only female contestant, I think."

"What do you mean…you think? Do I have a hired hand who isn't a man?"

"I'm not sure. Do you know who Daniel is?" Lucy asked.

Cal's brow furrowed as he tried to place the name. "Short, kind of skinny, quiet guy with glasses?"

"That's the one. I think he may be Danielle instead of Daniel."

Cal thought about that for a minute. "What exactly does that mean?"

"It means you have a 'cowgirl' working for you but she's afraid to let anyone know, so she's pretending to be a male so she can work here."

"Why didn't you tell me about this before this morning?"

"I forgot about it, honestly. But what difference does it make? If she can do the work, who cares?"

Cal frowned at her, "I think I might care if she's pretending to be someone she isn't."

Lucy shook her head. "We can discuss this later. Right now, I have a contest to win, my love." She kissed him and headed out the door.

* * *

The guys had done a good job of building a makeshift arena with portable gates fastened together to make the corral. Targets were put up for the rifle and the pistol competitions. The calves for roping were in one corral, and the larger cattle for cutting were in another. There were tables of food and drinks available. This had turned out to be a holiday in the midst of weeks of hard work for most of the men. Some of them brought their families.

Lucy was impressed. When Ben was in charge of something, he obviously enjoyed doing it right.

The first event was rifle accuracy. There were 10 people signed up to compete in the two parts. The first was standing and shooting at a target. The second was shooting from the back of a moving horse.

Lucy went looking for Len. She held out her hand and said, "Good luck, Len."

He shook her hand unenthusiastically and answered, "Yeah."

Lucy placed fourth in the stationary rifle and third in the moving portion of it. Len placed first in each category and was grinning from ear to ear.

It felt good to have her worst skill out of the way. She placed first in the pistol competition as Cal knew she would.

She wasn't the fastest in the roping, but her time was faster than Len's. The cutting competition was going to take place after lunch. Lucy switched saddles for this and watched as the herd of cattle was brought into the arena. She was checking the details of each animal. She wanted to choose the best one to "cut" from the herd. Choosing one on the edge was a reduction in points.

When it was her turn, Lucy rode Rigbee deep into the herd and selected the cow she wanted to cut or separate from the rest. When she got it out and away from the herd, she dropped a rein to let Rigbee take over and cut back and forth, twist and turn, and nearly set back on his rear end to stay in front of "his" cow and keep it separated, not allowing it to return to the herd.

It was hard work for horse and rider; it was difficult to stay in the saddle with the horse's sudden jerks and changes of direction. Each contestant had to "cut" three times, and the final score was an average of the three.

A few of the men couldn't keep their cow from returning to the herd. Len lost points when he selected a cow on the edge of the herd, but most did an exceptional job.

When the scores from the four competitions were added and averaged, a cowboy named Joe was the overall winner, Lucy was third and Len placed fourth. *Daniel* placed sixth.

Lucy congratulated Daniel and asked, quietly, "Why don't you want anyone to know you are a girl?"

Daniel's eyes opened wide, "Please don't tell, Mrs. Frasier. I'll lose my job. I knew they wouldn't hire me if I applied as a female, so I thought I could pull it off. I mean, I'm not very big in the girly places, you know?"

Lucy laughed at her terminology and assured her she would not lose her job. "I promise I will not let you lose your job, especially since you have proven your abilities today. Besides, I have some sway with the boss."

It was hot, hard work but a fun day, and Lucy was still excited as she made her way home. After she took care of Rigbee, she took a shower, poured an iced tea, and sat on the front porch swing to wait for Cal.

She heard a truck, but when she looked up, she was surprised to see Len haul his long legs out of the driver's side and walk up to the porch. He removed his hat and said, "I came by to say congratulations. You did a right fine job today, and I'm not too old or stubborn to say you beat me, fair and square. I apologize for saying a woman shouldn't go along."

"Apology accepted, Len. Sit down…would you like a cold drink?"

"No, thank you. I have to get going." He turned to leave, and then turned back. "I have to ask…how long you been ridin' like that?"

Lucy smiled, "Since my grandpa put me on a horse and taught me to rope and cut cattle. I was 6, I think, the first time I went on a round-up."

"No wonder," was his only comment as he walked down the steps.

* * *

Cal came home later and sat beside her. "You looked good out there, Baby. But I knew you would."

"Thanks, Boss Man. I spoke to Daniel, or really Danielle, today. She seems to think she'll lose her job if you find out she's a female. I assured her that wouldn't happen, and I had some sway with the boss."

"Think so?"

"I certainly hope so," she told him.

* * *

"Why are you walking like you're stiff?" Phoebe asked when she and Jerry joined Cal and Lucy for dinner after church on Sunday.

"I am stiff...everywhere," Lucy laughed. She proceeded to explain the contest that took place the previous day. "I hear we're going to Chicago for some Christmas shopping. Do you remember where you stored your boots, gloves, and winter coat?"

"I do. It hasn't been that long ago I was wearing them," Phoebe said. "I'm excited about the trip."

* * *

"I think I really am getting old, Cal, or I've been punishing my body too much lately. Between the week of cooking and yesterday's workout, I feel like I've been run over by a truck."

Cal proceeded to massage her neck and arms and legs and back. "Mmmm, that feels heavenly. If you decide to give up being a rancher, perhaps you could become a masseur."

"I wouldn't make much money. I'd only want to have one customer."

* * *

While she was looking for some winter things for the trip, Lucy decided to clean her closet, getting rid of all the clothes she no longer had an occasion to wear. She stood on a stepstool to reach the top shelf. As she leaned to reach the farthest corner, her foot slipped and she landed on her right arm. She checked all bones and declared herself okay, except for her wrist. It was beginning to swell and hurt.

She called Lynne, hoping she was home. When she answered, Lucy asked, "Lynne, could you take me to the emergency clinic? I don't want Candy to have to pack up Luke. I think I may have broken my wrist."

* * *

When the doctor read the x-rays, he told her, "It isn't broken, but it is a bad sprain. We'll wrap it to keep the swelling down and give you some pain medication. Try to keep it above your heart and apply ice."

"Are you in that much pain, Lucy?" Lynne asked when she saw tears silently coursing down her cheeks.

"Not physical pain. Disappointment pain," Lucy told her. "I was looking forward to going along on the fall round-up in a week." She sighed.

When they returned home, Lynne made sure she was comfortable on the couch where she could keep her arm aloft.

That's where Cal found her when he came home. "What's going on?" he asked.

"Nothing. Absolutely nothing is going on, including my going on that round-up," Lucy told him.

He sat down next to her and tried to console her. He wiped her tears and reminded her there would be the spring round-up.

"I don't want to go in the spring; I want to go *now*. How clumsy can I be? Ride all day a few days ago and then fall off a stepstool?"

"Lucy, you sound like a toddler having a tantrum."

"I *am* having a tantrum, thank you, so leave me alone, okay?" She stomped out of the room and slammed the door.

Cal made a cup of coffee and watched the news. He knew she would get over it, eventually.

An hour later, he knocked on the bedroom door and cracked it open. "Is it safe to come in or are you going to throw something at me?" he asked.

"No, I won't be throwing anything at you, Cal. Come in."

He sat on the bed next to her. "I'm sorry you're disappointed, Lucy. If I could fix it, I would."

"I know you would. It isn't just the round-up; it's the thought of being 60. This is what happens when people get old. They get clumsy and fall and break things, like bones."

He smiled at her. "First of all, you are not old, by any stretch of the imagination. You are the youngest, healthiest, most vibrant and beautiful "almost-60" person I know."

"You're prejudiced."

"Maybe…but it's still true. Let me fix you something to eat, and we'll continue this discussion, all right?"

As they ate, Cal told her, "I won't go on the round-up if you can't go, Lucy. There are plenty of capable men…and now a woman, too…who can take care of things. Ben will be there. They don't need me."

"Don't be silly, Cal. I want you to go. I promise I'll stop acting like a spoiled brat. Besides, it's important for the men to see the *boss* out there working with them. Please go."

Under protest, he did go for the first few days but returned in the middle of the third day. As he hung his hat up and took off his dusty work boots, he said, "They all know the old man can still handle a rope and separate cows, so I figured I could come home now to be with you."

* * *

The children and grandchildren came for cake and ice cream before Lucy's actual birthday in November. She asked for no gifts so the little ones drew pictures to be displayed on the front of the refrigerator, and Gabe used his signing skills to say, *Happy Birthday, Grandma.*

Her wrist was still wrapped when they boarded the plane for Chicago, but her attitude was much better.

* * *

Cal accompanied Jerry on some business errands while Phoebe and Lucy drove to Batavia to talk to Anna about purchasing the building Lucy owned. As soon as she saw her, Phoebe asked, "What on earth happened to you?" indicating the cut and bruising on Anna's face.

"I tripped and fell into the doorframe," Anna explained. "I'm not sure what I tripped on, maybe my own feet," she laughed.

Lucy held up her bandaged arm. "I fell off a stepstool."

They briefly discussed some options for Anna to purchase the store. Lucy told her to think about it, and they would speak again after the first of the year.

When they were on their way back to meet the men, Phoebe observed, "She didn't trip on anything. I would bet my last dollar she's in an abusive relationship."

Lucy asked, "How can you be so sure, Phoebe?"

"I recognized the look in her eyes when she was trying to explain it. I did that same thing a thousand times."

* * *

They were staying at one of Chicago's most luxurious hotels that exuded elegance and luxury from the opulent lobby to the indoor pool and tastefully decorated rooms. The four of them walked to the Michigan Avenue Bridge and shopped at the stores on the Magnificent Mile. Every tree on Michigan Avenue was adorned in tiny, twinkling lights, and the automated displays in the store windows were beautiful. As nighttime approached, light snowflakes began to fall, which turned the scene into a magical fairyland. It was overwhelmingly romantic, and the two couples stood and kissed like they were standing under the mistletoe.

"You won't enjoy a scene like this in Texas," Phoebe stated.

"I propose we bring these two lovely ladies here every year at this time," Cal told Jerry.

"I think that's a fantastic idea," Jerry agreed. "They can get their winter 'fix' and then we can go home where it's warm."

After they warmed up, they got dressed for the evening. "I should have taken my dress along to the doctor's office and asked for a matching wrap for my wrist. I hate not being color coordinated," Lucy quipped as she came out of the bedroom. "Cal, can you please zip up my dress? I can't do it with one hand."

Cal sucked in his breath when he saw her. "You look gorgeous, Lucy. I don't have enough words in my vocabulary to tell you how beautiful you are. Do you think Jerry and Phoebe would notice if we skipped dinner and stayed in our room all night?"

"I think they might notice, Cal. Besides, aren't you hungry? It's been a long day with very little food."

"I am truly hungry, Lucy, but food isn't going to satisfy me." He kissed the back of her neck after he zipped the dress, then turned her around and kissed her passionately. "Are you sure you want to go out for dinner?" he asked, as he sang the words to her favorite song in her ear: 'I can't believe how much it turns me on, just to be your man.'"

"Now you're not playing fair," she told him. "Come on, we have the whole night ahead of us, and they're practically newlyweds yet, so I'm sure they won't mind coming back early."

Dinner was extravagant, the dancing was fun, the conversation was interesting, and the wine was cold.

"Have you told her about her gift yet?" Jerry asked Cal.

"No, not yet, but I guess now is as good a time as any," Cal said.

He took her hands in his. "Lucy, you know we talked about combining the two ranches under one name. I've been talking to the real estate attorney, and he's drawn up the papers. Instead of making them into one ranch, I told him I wanted to keep them separate but change the Benson Ranch to the Yellow Rose. You would have the Yellow Rose Ranch back, Lucy."

Chapter 29

LUCY'S SMILE FADED, and she shook her head. "No, Cal. No, you can't do that. Is it already done?"

"He's just waiting for us to sign the papers. I don't understand, Lucy. I thought you would be pleased."

"I can't talk about this right now. Can we go back to the hotel, please?"

After they left, Jerry looked at Phoebe questioningly. "Do you have any idea what that was all about?" he asked.

Phoebe shook her head. "Not a clue. I used to think if she ever had a chance to have that ranch back, she would be in heaven. Obviously, I was wrong."

Phoebe changed the subject, "Jerry, I've wanted to ask you something. When you first met Lucy on the plane, were you attracted to her?"

Jerry smiled at her. "Yes, as a matter of fact, I was. I thought she was an articulate, attractive, obviously successful woman who was comfortable in her own skin, and that appealed to me. When we met again a few days later at a karaoke club, I saw the immediate chemistry between her and Cal and knew I didn't stand a chance."

"So, should I be offended or feel like second choice for you?"

"Absolutely not, Phoebe. God always knows what he is doing. Lucy would have challenged me every day of our lives together. Heck, she challenges me every time she's in my office, and we're *not* married," he laughed. "Living with her, I think, must be like watching a hurricane touch land. Cal is the perfect person for her as she is for him. He is the *calm,* and she is the *storm*. It seems they almost know what the other one is thinking. They complement each other in every way."

He continued, "You, however, are the perfect person for me, Phoebe, and I hope I am always that perfect person for you." He kissed her and said, "Let's go back to the hotel. I'm sure they will have everything straightened out by morning."

* * *

Lucy didn't say a word on the way back to their room. When they got there, she stood in the dark room looking out the window at the Chicago skyline. Cal took her coat and then stood behind her with his arms around her.

"Before you say anything, Cal, I need to say some things. I need to try to make you understand why I can't accept your gift; why I don't even want your gift."

She stepped out of his embrace and moved closer to the window. Cal sat down in a chair to listen to her explanation.

"Have you ever put a large jigsaw puzzle together? The kind you know is going to take weeks to complete because there are so many pieces and most of them look the same. You know what the finished picture should look like because it's on the front of the box, and as you work, you look at that picture often to make sure you're doing it right. My grandparents and the Yellow Rose were, in my mind, what my completed puzzle should look like. When I married John and we had children, the picture changed a bit, but the ranch was still there as the frame. When John died and then Leon lost the Yellow Rose, all the pieces I had put together suddenly were torn apart. So, I started a new picture, one that didn't depend on anyone but me. I was in charge of my 'puzzle' so to speak. I liked it that way, although there were always a few pieces missing and the Yellow Rose was still there in the background." She took a deep breath and moved away from the window.

"When I met you, I felt as though my puzzle was going to finally be complete. Then when I found out you were the one who owned the Yellow Rose, I not only tore the pieces apart, I threw them all over the floor. I decided I would start from square one: new puzzle, new picture, new pieces. When you came back into my life and we were married, that should have completed the puzzle, but every time I stepped back into my old life, I took some of the pieces with me. Anthony told me I had to stop stepping across the invisible line or I would lose you and possibly, my life. Then when I went to Colorado, Leon talked to me for a long time. He said I needed to let go of my longing for my life on the ranch. It was over, and while I would always have the memories, it was time to move on or it would destroy me."

"When I thought you were going to die and all I had left of you was your blood on my hands, I knew he was right. I had been going in both directions and never putting the last piece in the puzzle. I don't want any part of me to be separate from you. I know you wanted to make me happy by giving me the Yellow Rose name back, but I don't want it, Cal. It's part of my past." She turned to him and with tears in her eyes, said, "You are the puzzle piece that completes the picture of my life. Please don't take a piece out again and separate us in any way."

Cal stood and drew her into his embrace. "I'm sorry, Lucy. I should have seen how things had changed and realized you no longer spoke of the Yellow Rose as though it was some place you longed for. Can we keep the name on the cabin where we spent our wedding night?"

"Of course, and you know I will never part with my yellow rose diamond," she told him.

He unzipped her dress for her and kissed the tattoo of a yellow rose on the top of her left breast. "I believe it's nearly impossible to erase a tattoo," he stated.

"Mmmm, maybe I should get an 'F' for Frasier on the other side," Lucy suggested.

"That won't be necessary, Lucy. I know you belong to me and I belong to you, and no one is going to take any pieces out of your puzzle…ever again."

When they met for breakfast the next morning, Lucy apologized to Jerry and Phoebe. "I'm sorry for leaving last night. I can only say I was totally surprised, and while I have kept my memories of the Yellow Rose, it no longer rules supreme in my life. I don't want to have a separate ranch name. I want it all to be the Frasier Ranch because that's who I am. Having said that, let's discuss where we're going today."

They wandered in and out of stores, again enjoying the Christmas decorations and the lights. They ate lunch at the Rainforest Café and had as much fun as the children who were there.

"There's a jewelry store I want to visit, if y'all don't mind," Lucy said.

Jerry looked at Cal and winked. "This could be our undoing, my friend."

When they entered, a short, gray-haired man in a business suit immediately came from behind the counter and approached Lucy. He grabbed her hand and a smile spread across his face. "Miss Louisa. It is so good to see you. Where have you been? Ohhh, I have some new pieces I think you will like."

Lucy chuckled. "I'm sure you do, Vincent. But first, I want you to meet my husband, Calvin Frasier. And these are our friends, Jerry and Phoebe Watkins. Everyone, this is Vincent. I used to be a very good customer of his."

They shook hands. When Vincent saw Lucy's yellow diamond, he looked at Cal, "I see someone else has excellent taste in diamonds. Now, what can I do for you today?"

Lucy opened her bag and took out a velvet case. Opening it, she placed the contents on the glass counter. "Do you remember these, Vincent?"

"Oh, my, yes. These are exquisite pieces. Do they need to be repaired?"

"No, actually, I want to know if you can take them apart and make five cross necklaces out of the diamonds. They don't have to match, but they need to be similar in size. I want them for my daughters."

"Yes, I believe it can be done. Are you certain you want to take these apart? They are beautiful. You could buy five new necklaces for your daughters," Vincent told her.

"I could, but I have no use for these, and I would like to use them for something new. The catch, my friend, is this. I would like them for Christmas presents. Can it be done in time?"

Vincent raised his eyebrows. "That isn't much time. But for you, Louisa, I will do it. They will be ready by Christmas."

They left the store and decided to have a cup of coffee. Jerry asked, "I guess it's the lawyer in me, but did Vincent give you a receipt for that jewelry, Lucy? I'm not a diamond expert, but that looked like thousands of dollars' worth of diamonds to me."

"No, he didn't, but it's okay. Vincent and I have done a lot of business over the years. I trust him implicitly, and he knows I probably put his kids through college…singlehandedly," Lucy laughed.

Cal teased her, "You know it does scare a man a little bit when his wife is on a first name basis with a high-end jeweler."

* * *

On the flight home, Cal asked, "Lucy, why did you decide to get rid of some of your jewelry? You like all the pieces; I know you do."

"You're right, I do love beautiful jewelry, but I wanted to give the girls something special for Christmas. Besides, it doesn't fit my lifestyle any longer. Diamonds don't go too well with jeans and boots. I will keep a few pieces for special occasions, but I don't need jewelry on a daily basis. Phoebe has been considering opening a clothing store for abused women. Many of them leave home with nothing but the clothes on their back. It's a cause that's close to her heart. If I can sell some of my pieces, except for a few sentimental ones, I'll give her the money to start stocking her store if she proceeds with the idea."

She placed her hand in Cal's. "At one point in my life, my clothes and my jewelry defined me. They don't any longer."

* * *

The entire family celebrated Thanksgiving at Paul and Lynne's house. Sometime in the afternoon, Lucy found the children seated in a semi-circle in front of Cal, with Olivia and Luke in their carriers in front of the older children. Cal was playing his guitar very softly and singing "Jesus Loves Me" to them. The older ones were singing with him, and the babies were mesmerized by his voice. Vicki took a picture of the scene, and for once no one was making silly faces.

Gary made the announcement their expected baby was a boy, and they would name him Michael. With Gabe on his lap, he said, "Then we will have a Gabriel and a Michael…both archangels named in the Bible."

Gabe climbed down from Gary's lap and walked toward Cal. He put his hands on Cal's face and said, audibly, "Grandpa." The room was totally quiet. Jackie cried on Gary's shoulder, and Cal looked as though he might cry, too. Lucy looked at him across the room and smiled. *What a wonderful Thanksgiving gift,* she thought.

* * *

"Candy, I want to take you away for a weekend to celebrate our anniversary. Where would you like to go?" Ben asked.

"Well, my dear, there aren't too many romantic places to take a nursing baby."

"I know. I'll ask Dad and Lucy to watch Luke for the weekend. We have some frozen breast milk they can use. I know they will agree; they drop in to see him nearly every day."

Candy thought about that. "Oh, Ben, I don't know if I can be away from him that long."

Ben took her in his arms, "Yes, you can. I'll do my best to fill the time with excitement."

"I have no doubt of that, Ben. Just make sure we don't get started on the remainder of the dozen children Lucy thinks we should have," Candy warned as she pulled him in and kissed him.

* * *

Lucy watched as Cal held Luke and gave him his bottle. "Were you this involved with your children when they were babies?"

"I'd like to think so, but if Kathy were here, she'd probably disagree," Cal answered.

"I wish I had jumped on that horse with the 'Pony Express delivery man' that day so long ago. We could have made lots of babies together."

Cal laughed at her. "Or…maybe not. We weren't the same people then that we are today. I believe we needed all the experiences in our lives to become the people who fit so well together now."

"I suppose you're right. I certainly wasn't the same person then that I am now."

* * *

The Christmas tree was put up in the great room and the lights strung on it. Before any ornaments were hung, Lucy sat on the floor in front of it and, in the stillness of the night, contemplated all the events that had taken place since last Christmas when they were in the house in Illinois. Cal came out of their house and into the great room to join her, wearing only a pair of pajama bottoms.

Lucy smiled at him. "Do you remember when you stayed at my house in Batavia and you came to the kitchen with no shirt on? You said you packed in such a hurry, you forgot it. I remember almost dropping the empty cup I was holding when I saw you. I want you to know, Calvin Frasier, looking at you right now affects me exactly the same way it did then."

"That's good to know. I hope I affect you like that forever, Lucy Mae." He stretched out on the floor and pulled her down beside him so he could put his arms around her. "So tell me what you're thinking, sitting here in the dark, staring at the lighted tree."

"I'm thinking how blessed I am and how many things have transpired since last Christmas and wondering what another year will bring."

"It's probably a good thing God doesn't allow us to see the future. We might decide we don't want to participate in his plans for our lives."

Lucy turned to him and kissed him. "As long as you're in my life, Cowboy, I'm ready for anything.

Keep Reading for a Sneak Peek of *Riding With a Cowboy*, Book Three in the Magnolia Series

Chapter 1

CAL'S INNER ALARM CLOCK woke him as it had nearly every day of his life since he was in high school. He extricated himself from his curled up position around Lucy's body, trying not to disturb her. He sat on the edge of the bed for a bit before pulling on some pajama pants and going to the tiny kitchen in their shore-side cabin to make coffee.

When he came back to the bedroom, he drank his coffee while he watched Lucy sleep. Her bare shoulders above the edge of the sheet were tanned and smooth. Looking at her reminded him of their time together last night. Her dark hair was fanned out on the white pillow; her breathing was peaceful while a slight smile seemed to play around her lips. Perhaps she was dreaming of the last two weeks they shared on this island getaway. It was a trip he planned for their second anniversary, and he had actually been able to keep it a secret and surprise her.

The days had flown by, each one more exciting and fun than the one preceding it. Going back to their cattle and horse ranch in Texas might be anticlimactic after two weeks of perfect bliss.

Lucy stirred, rolled onto her back and opened her eyes. "What are you doing, Cal?" she asked sleepily when she saw him sitting in a chair, gazing at her.

"Looking at the most gorgeous woman in the world while she sleeps," was his reply.

Lucy started laughing and wiped her cheek. "I think the most gorgeous woman in the world drools when she sleeps," she said.

Cal smiled and held out a cup of coffee for her. "I don't mind."

Lucy sat up, pulling the sheet up a bit and reached for the cup. "You are way too good to me, Cowboy. You've had coffee ready for me every day since we got married, with the exception of when you were in the hospital after being shot, of course."

"Making coffee is such a small thing, Lucy. I would do anything in the world for you, and you know that, right?"

"Yes, I do know that. And your actions make me aware of that every day."

He moved to the bed and kissed her. "This is our last day in paradise," he told her. "What would you like to do today?"

"I think we've taken advantage of everything that's offered—scuba diving, horseback riding on the beach, deep-sea fishing, snorkeling, sailing, our version of tennis," Lucy chuckled, "and a trip through the casinos. I almost forgot, we went canoeing, too."

"It has been fun, hasn't it? Even though you refused to go parasailing," Cal told her.

"I didn't stop you from going, Sweetheart. I just said I wasn't doing that. Not in a million years."

"I think we ate our way through the two weeks, too. I haven't eaten that much or that variety of delicious food in a long time."

Lucy held the sheet back. "Why don't you get back under the sheets with me, and we'll discuss what we're going to do today, okay?"

Cal put his coffee cup down and climbed back in bed. "So tell me, Lucy Mae," he asked as he waited for her to snuggle up to him and put her head on his shoulder, "what would be the best thing to do on our last day here?"

"I want to walk along the water's edge and say our morning prayers while we walk," Lucy began. "Then I want to buy a basket of the fresh fruit they have at the stand with the thatched roof and then…I don't know, I'm sure we'll think of some other activity while we walk."

She kissed him and headed to the shower, wrapping the bed sheet around herself and taking it with her as she went.

"What's up with the sheet wrapped around you, Lucy?" Cal laughed.

"I've always wanted to do that. You know, like women do in the movies—wrap themselves in the sheet as they walk away from the bed," Lucy told him. "I can't do that at home because then I'd have to put a new sheet on the bed. This was my chance. Here, someone else will replace the sheets."

* * *

"If you want, I'll spread some sunscreen on your shoulders and back, Cal," Lucy said, "but I don't want any today. My shoulders are still sore from yesterday. The straps of my bathing suit even make them hurt. I'll put a lightweight t-shirt on instead. That should protect me from the inevitable sunburn. I don't usually burn, but obviously the sun is different here."

They walked barefoot along the water's edge. The sand was warm even this early in the morning, and the small waves danced at their feet as they strolled, hand in hand. The turquoise water was as clear as glass for a long distance from shore. Where it became a little deeper, the color changed to an azure blue. The beach was nearly deserted, and everything was quiet with the exception of the birds circling and the soft gurgle of the water as it lapped the sand.

Cal and Lucy said their morning prayers as they did every day, almost as a conversation with God. Cal had done this since he accepted Christ on a mission trip when he was in college. Lucy had to learn to "talk" to God again, after turning her back on him for many years. In her wedding vows, she said God led her into Cal's arms and Cal led her back into the arms of her Savior. She meant it that day and still felt that way. Now, she couldn't imagine a day without God in it.

They began their conversation with God by giving thanks for every blessing in their lives: their grown children and grandchildren, their friends, and the everyday blessings of health and prosperity, love and laughter, the wonders of new babies in their family, and his protection in every area of their lives. Included in their prayers were specific requests for various people and situations. They asked for God's blessings on their ranch and their employees, their church family, the country, and its leaders.

This shared prayer time was one more thing in their lives that bound them together and increased their feelings of being one person, in thought, actions and feelings.

"Are you certain you don't want to take this last opportunity to try parasailing, Lucy?" Cal laughingly asked when they finished their prayers.

She shaded her eyes and watched as some fearless soul sailed over them. "Nope. I will never regret not doing that. Thank you, anyway."

As she was looking up, she lost her footing in the sand and stumbled backward. Before Cal could catch her, she landed in the water. She grabbed Cal's arm and pulled him in with her. "Come with me. We may as well enjoy this gorgeous day and the water for a bit before we have to leave it all behind."

They walked out until the water was deep enough for swimming, then they swam for a while before walking back to the shoreline. When Lucy put the t-shirt on she had not planned on getting wet or swimming and only became self-conscious of how it was clinging to her body when she saw the appreciative look on Cal's face as she walked out of the water.

"Come on, Sweetheart," she said as she grabbed his hand and hurried toward their cabin. "This is not a good thing."

Cal laughed at her, "Lucy, there's no one out here but the two of us, and I think you would win a wet T-shirt contest any day of the week." As they walked, Cal asked her again what she would like to do on their last day of vacation.

"I want to do something you suggested a long time ago."

"I suggested it?" Cal asked, puzzled. "What was that?"

"Do you remember when it seemed like everything that could possibly go wrong…was going wrong?" Lucy asked him. "The rustling scheme was a huge concern, Jackie was upset about Gabe's autism diagnosis, and Samantha's marriage seemed to be falling apart?"

"Yes," Cal said slowly. "But I don't remember what I said I wanted."

"This is a quote, my dear. You said, 'I want just one day to not think about any of those things. I want to get up in the morning, drink coffee with you, ride Cutter for a little while, and then come home and make love to you all day long, with no phone calls or visits from anyone.'"

Cal nodded. "I do remember saying that. I was feeling overwhelmed by life and wanted… no, *needed…* a respite with you in my arms all day."

Lucy smiled at him and looked into his eyes. "We've already had our coffee, we've walked in the sand in place of riding Cutter, and now we're back here. We can turn our phones off and spend the rest of our last day together, uninterrupted. How does that sound, Cowboy?"

Cal pulled her to him, removed the wet T-shirt and kissed her in a way that answered her question.

Made in the USA
Charleston, SC
07 November 2016